T0149508

PICTURE
JESUS

LINDA BISHOP

WESTBOW
PRESS®
A DIVISION OF THOMAS NELSON
& ZONDERVAN

THE HOLY BIBLE, NEW INTERNATIONAL VERSION®,
NIV® Copyright © 1973, 1978, 1984, 2011 by Biblica, Inc.®
Used by permission. All rights reserved worldwide.

WestBow Press books may be ordered through booksellers or by contacting:

WestBow Press
A Division of Thomas Nelson & Zondervan
1663 Liberty Drive
Bloomington, IN 47403
www.westbowpress.com
1 (866) 928-1240

Because of the dynamic nature of the Internet, any web addresses or
links contained in this book may have changed since publication and
may no longer be valid. The views expressed in this work are solely those
of the author and do not necessarily reflect the views of the publisher,
and the publisher hereby disclaims any responsibility for them.

Any people depicted in stock imagery provided by Thinkstock are models,
and such images are being used for illustrative purposes only.
Certain stock imagery © Thinkstock.

ISBN: 978-1-5127-7902-8 (sc)
ISBN: 978-1-5127-7904-2 (hc)
ISBN: 978-1-5127-7903-5 (e)

Library of Congress Control Number: 2017903899

Print information available on the last page.

WestBow Press rev. date: 03/15/2017

CONTENTS

1   *It started in a dream*—**In the Beginning** 1

2   *For Worry*—**The Gift** 5

3   *For Healing*—**The Healer** 9

4   *For Controlling Pain*—**The Creator Throws You The Sun** 16

5   *God With Us*—**In the Hands of God** 23

6   *Fear*—**The Protector God** 28

7   *For growth, to become a new creation, making change, for transformation*— **You Are the Pot** 31

8   *Care of the Sick*—**He Touched Me** 36

9   *For Protection*—**The Armor of God** 43

10   *For Knowing Gifts*—**How Am I Gifted?** 48

11   *For Belonging to God, Following Jesus*— **Bicycle Built for Two** 52

12   *Anger*—**The Weight on Your Shoulders** 56

13   *For Receiving forgiveness*—**Take It--It's Yours** 62

14   *For Forgiving Others*—**The Big Bully** 65

15   *For Self-Acceptance*—**Self-image** 68

16   *For Friends, Support, Trust*—**I Call You Friend** 74

17   *For Loneliness, Friendliness*—**Make New Friends** 80

18   *Jesus to the Rescue*—**Searching for The Face** 90

19   *Fear of the Unknown*—**Let Go and Let God:
The New Bicycle**...**93**

20   *For Protection, Direction*—**Touch of God** **99**

21   *For Service, Call to Ministry*—**You Do It Unto Me**.........**103**

22   *For Concern for Others, Intercessory Prayer*—
Jesus, Help! **108**

23   *For Prayer*—**Lord, Teach Me to Pray**............................**114**

24   *Abundant Welcome*—**Welcome! Come on in!** **119**

25   *Tears*—**The Desert** **123**

ONE

IT STARTED IN A DREAM

In the Beginning

I longed for time with Jesus, time when he was all mine and I was all his, time so different from everyday life, hectic and stress filled. I longed for a way to be with him. I longed for a way to sit with him and share my joys and problems and concerns and the daily ills of everyday living.

One day last winter, after a particularly hectic day in the church office, on the freeway, in the hospital, leading a funeral, I talked to God about it in the standard way I talk with God, while I was driving on the freeway. *Dear God,* I began with the familiar address. How would God know it was me—I?—if I said something else. Some people say "Dear Jesus" or "Hello Jesus" or "Heavenly Father" or "Loving God" or some other address, but I've always wanted to keep it simple in private times, and I figure God knows to whom I am speaking. My old friend Ginger who ran the big Catholic church used to say, "Hi, Jesus, it's me," which was very much like her but not so much like me. So I just addressed God as always and began talking.

I've discovered that my most fulfilling prayer moments are when I don't do any asking or thanking or confessing or talking to God, but when I'm just in Jesus' presence—in the presence of God—when Jesus is with me, Julia. I struggle with problems, ills, and stresses as everyone does. I find I'm the most at one with God when I give God my problems, ills and stresses and just remain in the presence of the Lord.

Jesus tells us to pray always. How I wished I could and still be in the real world, living a real life full of other people, the vacillations of the economy, and the practicalities of living. I'd tried working on a better prayer life, taking more time out to study and read the words of the Bible and the writings of others more spiritual than I am. I'd tried weaving prayer into or on top of work and play and getting from one place to another. I'm happier when I have a fulfilling prayer life. I wanted to do better.

That thought sounds like I wrote it, doesn't it?—the long convoluted sentences, the repetition. That's just the way I talk—like I write—with dashes. In my life as a writer, sometimes in my mind, I would write myself comforting scenarios allowing me to meet with Jesus, giving him my problems, and then allowing him the space and time to do something about them. At first I had tremendous difficulty with this. I am usually a gentle, reasonable, flexible person, but like most people, I like to be in control, independent. It comes from my CEO background and directing plays. Sometimes, sorry to say, I'm like that with other people, even when it's not appropriate. And almost all of the time, I'm like that with myself. If I'm not multi-tasking, I'm berating myself for not. As a kid, if I wasn't earning A's, I was beating up on myself for a B+. In fifth grade I got all As on my report card, and my dad asked me what I was going to do now. Maybe he thought I peaked too soon. I still don't know for sure. Actually they had me skip half that year, straight to the sixth grade.

It was the same in seminary, which was even more stupid of me. I asked the Prof if I could write a play for the final paper as long as I kept the rule of sourcing at least half in original, primary sources. He liked that idea, so then I asked if he would push the length required from fifteen pages to forty-five, as I doubted if I could write a whole play in fifteen pages. His mouth dropped open, and he nodded his head. He liked the play and gave me an A. I guess I'm a bit of an overachiever.

If I'm not doing something all the time, I'm self-flagellating, and that takes up the spare moments.

Today I'm a minister, what is called a second-career minister. After years in a former career as a theater director and performer and television producer, scenes come naturally to me. In theater and film we see interaction between people as the mainstay for pushing forward the plot, developing character, resolving conflict and coming to denouement. That's life, and I'm used to the format. I'm also an English teacher who teaches playwriting, so I teach my students all that.

I'm telling you all of this, thinking maybe you are a little bit like me. Maybe you see life in scenes. Maybe you want a better relationship with God. Maybe you have daily problems, too, and ongoing life-problems, too. Maybe Jesus can help the both of us. I take that back. I am a minister, and I *know* that Jesus can help the both of us.

I credit Jesus with the process of figuring this out for myself and hope I have followed his promptings and honor him with following him. Acknowledging the depth of the challenges we all face, I'm humbled that Jesus listens to me and helps me to work on my issues. I have achieved a degree of solace through the grace of God for which I am thankful and at times amazed.

Back to my prayer on that winter day. It was a regular prayer

TWO

FOR WORRY

The Gift

"Peace I leave with you. My peace I give to you. I do not give to you as the world gives. Do not let not your hearts be troubled and do not be afraid." John 14:27

In a dream, of course, you don't know you are dreaming. It seems more like you are watching a movie you're in. In fact in some way, you play all the roles.

In the dream I first see a rock on the table in front of me. I somehow know this rock is my worry, that is, what I was worrying about earlier in the day when I was on the freeway. Somehow I know I should name this rock. I say to it, "This rock is MY WORRY."

I tell this rock what my worry is at that moment: my worry is that my mind is blank about what I should write for a sermon for Sunday because this day has been filled with freeways and office work, Jack in the hospital which was frightening, and a funeral.

It was as if I were writing a script in the dream; I knew that I should describe the rock. Is it a little, smooth, flat stone, the kind you might skip across the lake? Is it big...and jagged, full of sharp edges and dangerous points that stick out? Is it pretty like conglomerate or shale or a precious stone or marble? Or is it common, the color of ordinary dirt? It is gray and common and big enough to knock a hole in a skull.

I pick it up in my hands and feel how heavy it is. In the dream with no such thing as weight, the act seems meaningful to me. I put it down again.

Next to the rock on the table is a box that is just a little bit bigger than my rock. It is an ordinary box...not new...old...but not dilapidated...strong. I lift off the top of the box. The box is empty. I foolishly put my head inside and see that the box is empty.

I pick up the rock again and call it by its name again. I call it MY WORRY. Now I put the rock in the box and put the top on the box. I can't see my rock anymore, of course. No, now it is completely covered by the box.

I look across the table. There is somebody sitting on the other side of the table looking at me. He is smiling. It is Jesus.

What does he have in his hands? It's a box. But it doesn't look like my box. It's a package. It's all wrapped up like a gift. Like a birthday gift. Very frilly paper and ribbon. The kind you'd decorate for your best friend's birthday party when you're little.

Jesus puts his package, his gift, on the table in front of him. Then he smiles and pushes it halfway across the table toward me. He stops. Then he says to me, "Give me your package, and I will give you my package."

I wonder, Why does Jesus want my rock? Doesn't he know there's only a rock in this box? I push my box toward Jesus, and he pushes his box toward me. We trade boxes.

He doesn't look in my box. He says, "Open my package." I take off the lid and look inside. He says, "It's a gift." I know what it is, don't you? I know it's grace.

I look in the box. What do I see? What shape is it? What color is it? I reach into the box and lift it out. How big is it? How heavy is it? Is it soft, like cotton...or a cloud, or spun sugar that you buy at the carnival? I lift it up to my nose and smell it. What does it smell like? Flowers, strawberries, the earth, a cool wind? So much to remember about it. In my dream I put it on my chest...and I push it through my skin...into my heart.

I have a little left on my fingers. I put it on my forehead...and I push it through my skin...into my mind.

Jesus says to me, "Now you have the grace of Jesus in your heart and in your mind."

Jesus picks up my box with my rock in it. He gets up from the table, he smiles at me, and he walks away.

That was the dream. I know it was because, like a good writer, I rolled over to the drawer in the side table, took out my writer's pen and pad, and wrote it all down while I could remember it, or I never would have believed it myself.

In each dream I have had about Jesus, he is a bit different. I've seen him with and without specific facial features, strong or gentle, looking just like my favorite portrait of him that hung in my Sunday School room when I was eight, or in the stained glass window of my church, or in a children's book I loved at six years old, or some other way that was meaningful to me at the time. Sometimes he looks more like my Father or my favorite Profs at Seminary. That would make sense in a dream. Yet in the dream I always know that it is Jesus who is talking to me even if he looks like someone else I admire and respect.

I have come to know different answers from Jesus through the Holy Spirit. One day one answer works better than another, and cumulatively the answers work best as a whole. It might have something to do with spiritual maturity. I hope so.

THREE

FOR HEALING

The Healer

"He heals the brokenhearted and binds up their wounds."
Psalm 147:3

Jack, who was in the hospital that day, had yet another heart attack, a small one as a follow-up to the big one that sent me as the minister to the hospital to pray with him. Jack wasn't the oldest man in the church, only ninety-two. LaMar was older at 102. LaMar died the next day. I spent the rest of the day after the hospital visit with Jack, the night and the next day with LaMar and his family, talking, praying, dreaming. While I was just down the hall from Jack's room, he had another heart attack, a massive one, and died. I didn't know until I peeked into Jack's room after LaMar's death. Leaning against the wall next to Jack's empty bed, silent tears came.

The dreaming came as soon as I got home after death came. After some 36 hours of trauma and drama, I fell into the big white marshmallow of my bed and turned the electric blanket up to 9. It felt as if the dream came the moment I closed my eyes.

I was lying on the ground, half on my side and half on my stomach, almost like a baby in the fetal position, probably taken from the position of my body in the bed. My legs were pulled up under me. My arms were under me, and my hands covered my heart.

Something stuck out from between my fingers. It looked like an arrow. The arrow had pierced my heart and caused it to break. What was that arrow that had broken my heart? I whispered their names: Jack, LaMar.

Something felt wet. What was it? The blood from where the arrow had pierced? Or was it my tears? Did I cry from pain?

Someone came. I couldn't see him, but you know who it was. He called me by name, Julia. I could hear him saying my name, Julia. He sounded like Ginger when he said, "It's me. It's Jesus. I've come. I've come to help you."

Jesus put his hand on my cheek. It was cool against my skin. He wiped my tears and pushed back my hair like my mother used to when I was a child. He put his hand on my forehead as if he were feeling my temperature. His hand was light and gentle.

Jesus said, "Where are you hurt?"

I answered, "It's my heart. There is an arrow in my heart, and it's broken."

Jesus said, "Let me help you turn over so that I can see your arrow."

I burst out, "No, I don't want you to see it. I am ashamed."

He called my name again. He said, "Oh, dear. Don't you know that I have seen every arrow in every wound that ever existed? I am an experienced medical caregiver. I am an emergency medical technician. I am a doctor and a psychiatrist. I am a minister. I am a rabbi. I am your friend. I am your mother and your father. I do not judge you. I don't ask you why you have an arrow in your heart. I don't ask you to name your arrow. Now let me help you to turn over so that I can see your arrow."

Jesus put his hands on my shoulder and my hip and slowly and carefully helped me to turn to face him. *"I'm going to take the arrow from your heart,"* he said.

"No, no," I yelled. *"Won't it hurt? Won't I bleed to death if you take it out?"*

"No, it won't hurt," he said. *"I won't let it hurt when I take the arrow from you. You may bleed a little...but it will stop...soon enough."*

He put a strong hand around the arrow and lifted it as delicately as lifting a knife out of butter. *"How does it feel to you? It doesn't hurt, does it?"* In fact, there was relief of the pain that it was causing. There was a little blood that came from the wound, but Jesus put the heel of his hand on the wound and held it there. He pressed and held it still...for a long time...a long time.

"How long does it take?" I asked. *"How long will you hold it until you know the bleeding has stopped?"*

He took a cloth out from a fold in his robe. He touched it to my skin. It was soft. He ripped it into long strips like bandages, and he bound my chest with it. As he wrapped it around my heart, it caused a warmth over my heart. What was that warmth?

There were no fasteners on the wrap to make it stay. There was no adhesive to make it stick. Jesus merely touched it, and it stayed in place.

"How do you feel? How is your broken heart?" Jesus picked up the arrow and put it inside his garment. *"You can't see it any longer. It is no longer in your heart. I have healed you--the brokenhearted--and bound up your wounds."*

When I awoke, it was night again. It seemed it was right after Jesus left me after the dream, but it was likely hours and hours. Mark was curled up beside me, spooning, with a comforting arm around my heart. He hadn't shut the blinds when he'd come to bed without waking me, so I could see the stars in the black sky and the halo around the moon. I only looked for a moment before I closed my eyes again and drifted off.

Sitting beside a hospital bed wasn't anything new to me. Since I was sixteen and until my father's death when I was 38, there wasn't a year that went by that I hadn't rushed cross-country in answer to a call saying one or the other of either Mom or Dad was in the hospital. It got so that I was jealous of seeing families or couples aboard a plane who were obviously going to Disneyland or an ocean vacation because I knew I was going to yet another bedside. I sound very cold to myself now. I wasn't cold then. I was emotional, tearful, worried, scared, lonely. For a good number of those years, Dad was still working at Fox Studios before his retirement to take care of Mom fulltime. So the rush call would include the name of the hospital, and I would drive directly there from LAX in a rental car. That was the longest, loneliest part of the trip, completely alone, not knowing what I would see when I got there. Messages from Dad were always brief and to the point: "Julia, Mother's in the hospital again. Come."

I'd ask which hospital. He'd answer, usually, Santa Monica. I'd ask, "What happened?"

Dad would answer, "Same thing, only she got worse." That would not be an answer at all. It could mean that she's in a coma, or she lit herself on fire, or she fell and busted her wrist and her hand. That time when I got there, she was laying very still in the hospital bed, completely alone in the darkened room, an angelic look on her face with her hands folded on her chest like a corpse, but not dead at least, breathing loud and fast. I nearly jumped back physically.

No, not nearly—I did. I called her name—Mom—quietly but got no response. I settled in. The fast breathing continued. I tried to match mine to hers to see just how fast it was. I couldn't keep up. Her hands were still, but the top one was dark red and huge. I stared at it, hoping that would make a difference. It didn't.

The nurse walked in and spoke full voice. "Are you her daughter? We've been waiting for you. Your father's still at work." Of course, I thought. But I took it back quickly, remembering all the days and nights he took care of her and worked at the same time. "We're waiting for the hand surgeon, too. As soon as he gets here, we'll take her in."

"Hand surgeon? What's the matter with her hand?"

She looked at me like I was stupid, then took it back. "She tripped and fell, probably on her robe, and she fell on her hand. X-ray says she shattered her wrist—it's like little pebbles—and all the blood vessels ruptured. They all burst open. But the skin didn't. So it's like a big balloon full of blood. A regular surgeon can't fix it. Because it's so bad, none of 'em will touch it, so we have to wait for the hand surgeon. But he's very good. He'll do a good job."

"Of course," I thought. Or maybe I said it out loud. Santa Monica Hospital can get all the best physicians. That's not the concern, just one more thing that's trying to mend while the rest of the body is trying to mend, too, and doing a lousy job of it. It had been years of one thing after another with the best doctors in Los Angeles trying to figure it out. The latest try was against porphyria—acute intermittent porphyria, a rare tropical disease. No, she had not been to the tropics. With it comes severe abdominal pain with all the symptoms that cause that, always sending Mom to the bathroom and then to bed. High blood pressure, sweating, restlessness. Nerves that control the muscles can be damaged causing weakness in the shoulders and the arms. Then tremors and seizures. She had it all,

13

and more. That kind of pain led to what looked like a case of the nerves in the 1960's. So the doctors gave her pills—in the 1960's. I don't know which was worse—the pain or the pills. She had the effects of both. A side effect was that she was afraid to be alone. So to stay home and take care of her, Dad quit the job in the studio he'd had for 30 years just as soon as he finished the Batman movie. He had made the whole TV series. He was a key grip, the guy in charge of the set and special effects before special effects were created on a computer, and he specialized in the crab dolly and the boom. He was the best in the business, best in the industry. Over the years after that, they grew to need even more help and had nurses every afternoon so Dad could get some rest.

Her hand in distress was just another symptom in a long, long list: pebbles instead of a wrist, lots of pain, more painkillers, more stomach upset, a vicious circle. Dad kept their pills in a shoe box, then two shoeboxes, one for each of them. Dad had a pharmacist brother-in-law back east who would send them the really big bottles of drugs (rather meds), so they wouldn't run out as often.

Years later, about 1987, I was starting to show some of the symptoms. There were only two doctors in the United States who were specialists in porphyria, and one was at the hospital less than a hundred steps from my office. I took a whole series of tests. Plus a new one. He finally told me that yes, porphyria was genetic; yes, I could have "caught it" from my mother—if she had had it. But it was clear that she didn't. The new test cut out a lot of false positives; mine was one; likely she was mis-diagnosed. Then what did she have? It was 1987; she had died in 1980. Too late. Ten years later, I was diagnosed with fibromyalgia. Many of the symptoms are similar. From this far away, I would guess that Mom had a very bad case of fibromyalgia with symptoms multiplied by the drugs she took to "help" her.

14

I sound hardened. I had to be. Mom suffered for twenty years. I couldn't watch her pain every day for any length of time. I was grateful that it was required that I go back to school, that I get back to my job at the TV station, that I leave. Mom knew that. Dad didn't. And it was required that I come back when she got so bad that she was in the hospital again. She always got better when I came, until the last time. They had been at my house over Christmas for a grueling time. She felt awful. She was very ill. Her temper was short, and mine quickly grew to match it. She was not her sweet self, and though she knew it, she couldn't seem to get rid of her anger. Nothing pleased her. Not even her favorite shrimp and ice cream.

The next day she left, and the day after she called me from the Motion Picture home where they lived. That was a rare happening. She apologized for her nasty behavior. I apologized back. I tried to let her know that I understood, that the fault was mine, too. She wouldn't hear of it. She took the fault 100% on her own head. She told me she loved me. I told her I loved her. I don't remember who said it first. She died of a stroke the next day.

FOUR

FOR CONTROLLING PAIN

The Creator Throws You The Sun

"And God said, let there be lights in the expanse of the sky...and it was so. God made two great lights, the greater light to govern the day and the lesser light to govern the night." Genesis 1: 14-16

The next morning my body was tired but not in pain generally speaking, though it seemed my heart still hurt. Grief will do that. Sometimes you are numb for a long time after the grief-causing event. But in a minister's life, grief comes so often that we don't have as much time to hold onto it. However, there is a build up that comes in the heart that stifles, jams up like a river that gets jammed by a beaver building a dam. Sometimes someone or something happens to break it up, but more often it just wears away with the constant flow of water over it. Occasionally it breaks, and the floodgates open in tears or anger or terror or even craziness. But not so often. Usually I put my attention into a creative Sunday sermon to help wash it away slowly and in little pieces that aren't so harmful.

I did just that for the Sunday after losing LaMar and Jack. This is the metaphorical story I told in the sermon.

Picture the creation. God has separated the day from the night. God has separated the water from the expanse and the water from the dry ground. On that dry ground God has created vegetation, plants of all kinds. Now it is time to set the two great lights in the sky. To create the greater light, the sun, the Creator walks all over the earth collecting colors from the plants and flowers everywhere. Can you picture it? God gathers the brightest color from the yellow center in the daisy and from the yellow coreopsis. The Great Painter gathers blue from the larkspur and red from the rose. Those are the three primary colors from which all other colors can be made. But God doesn't stop there. God gathers the purple from the little purple pansy and orange from the day lily. The Green God gathers green from the foliage that surrounds all the flowers, holds them up and protects them.

God doesn't stop the search until all the shades of every color that are created on earth are gathered. From each of these plants and flowers, God takes a little of their color, and, like a painter, mixes the colors together in equal parts. What color does he get? The color of night. Black.

So God spreads this mix of color over the night sky and into it flings the moon, bright and shining and purely white. The night sky is a foil for its beauty.

Then God goes back to the flowers of all the colors of the world. This time the Creator doesn't mix the colors themselves, but the light that is reflected from each of the colors. Can you see how the light of yellow and the light of red make the light of orange?

Then God takes the lights from all the colors and mixes them together to get pure light, pure white, which is the light of all colors.

God dips the sun into the light of all colors, and when it comes out, it is pure white. God flings the sun into the sky and stands back to look at the white sun in the daytime sky. You might think the next words out of God's mouth would be, "It is good." But instead God says, "Not quite." You see, the sky is perfectly blue and the puffy clouds are perfectly white, but the sun doesn't stand out when it, too, is perfectly white. So God reaches down and picks up one little daisy, takes the light from the yellow center of the little daisy, reaches back and throws it at the sun, and the sun turns yellow—a perfect yellow—the color the sun should be. And then God says, "It is good."

You're smiling at the fantasy story I told in the sermon that you have pictured like a child pictures the stories about God. It's a sweet story, and it makes you happy as you get away from your body. But now come back to your body, like I did that afternoon after the sermon and after the music and after the death announcements and the sighs and the tears. I took to the chaise lounge under the tree in our backyard. The rest of the family had gone to Mom's for Sunday lunch. Mom would understand my not being there. Dad would pout. They would bring me a full plate of my favorites, but I needed to be alone with Jesus. I hurt everywhere. All over my body and especially in my heart.

How would I do this? Have you ever tried talking to yourself as if you are two people, the "counselor" and "the doer/patient/other"? I had often been the counselor and worked the interaction with a person in need of help. Now I just needed to play both parts. This is what I tried. I'll write it for you like a script in first person present tense as if you are actually there.

Me as Counselor: *No matter what position you are in, picture yourself stretched out on the floor or a bed. How does your body feel?*

As the Other: (Here I, as the other, think about how to answer and do so. The specific response is not important.)

Counselor: *Are you entirely comfortable? Or is there a pain somewhere? Where is that pain?* (I found the pain. I wanted to talk about the one in my heart.) *Name the pain.* (Grief.)

Can you isolate that pain? (I could. I did. I thought just of the pain in my heart.)

If you have more than one pain, let's look at one at a time.

As you isolate that pain away from the muscles around it, what color do you see that it is? Is it bright red and fiery? Is it bright yellow like a hot poker? Is it a dark purple or blue or deep green like a bruise? Is it a constant swirl of color that pulsates and wraps around itself, a pot of swirling molten color? Is it coal black that seems to have no light at all? (The color choice may indicate how old versus fresh the pain is, how intense, how critical. As the patient, I answered as "we" went. I chose hot poker.)

Picture now that God is standing at your feet. The Creator has the sun in hand. It is the color of the light of all colors. It swirls with the balanced light of all colors so that it is perfectly white. (Here I picked up what I had taught myself from the sermon—although I also credit the Holy Spirit for the teaching.) *God tosses it lightly to you, and you catch it, not with your hands, but with your lips. You taste the purity of the sun, a perfect mixture of all tastes. You taste that it is a little tart, and a little bitter, and a little sour, and mostly sweet. And after you taste it, you swirl it around in your mouth, and then you swallow it.* (I actually did the action of swirling the sun although I knew what the responses would be. Blending the two speakers yet keeping them separate is a challenge.)

It goes everywhere throughout your body. It goes into your stomach and throughout your belly. It goes into your heart and throughout your blood stream. (I tried to follow my words with thoughts of the Other, seeing the parts of the body in my mind's eye.) *Your bloodstream carries it to every muscle. It goes into your brain. And as it gathers into a thought in your brain, you are able to direct it. You send it to the pain.* (I aimed it at my heart.) *Now all the light and color that was all over your body is focused and settles at the point of your pain.* (Now I spoke more slowly and quietly.) *The light warms the pain, breaks it up, and releases it. The color absorbs the color of the pain—like dark is absorbed by the light--and leaves in its place pure color. The color flows out the ends of your toes and the ends of your fingers, and you purse your lips and blow out the last of the color like you are blowing a kiss.* (I did.)

God watches as you do this. As you blow the kiss, God catches it in his hand. And God rolls it around like a ball in the hand. (I stole this image from James Weldon Johnson from his Negro preacher telling his version of *"The Creation"* in the poem of the same name. He rolls the mud around in his hand to make a man.) *Then God tosses it back to you, and you catch it with your lips. God does this as many times as you need it until the color has absorbed all of the pains from your body.*

I slipped into sleep again with the sun on my toes. I woke when the sun reached the top of my legs. Warmth from the sun on my tanning legs changed the feeling in the bottom half of my body. I laid there looking at the dappled shadows until the warmth had reached my chin. I tossed the kiss from me to God and back again many times until all the pain was absorbed from my body.

In another dream I was in the kitchen with my Mom. I was a kid, less than fourteen because we moved when I was fourteen, and this was the kitchen I grew up in where I stood on a chair to dry the dishes from age three, and we sang 20's and 30's era top ten hits. I knew all the words, too. You see my Mom and her sister Millie had sung on the radio in Salt Lake City when they were teenagers and headed to Hollywood as soon as they graduated high school, to break into the movies. The locals loved them. Why shouldn't Hollywood?

There we were. But I wasn't on the chair. I was on the floor next to Mom, singing and dancing the Charleston.

Water was dripping down her elbows as she swung her arms. As she kicked her right foot forward, she would kick me on the bum, and I'd let out a peal of laughter. We sang together, "Won't you Charleston with me? Won't you Charleston with me?"

FIVE

GOD WITH US

In the Hands of God

"So, do not fear for I am with you;
Do not be dismayed for I am your God.
I will strengthen you and help you,
I will uphold you with my righteous right hand." Isaiah 41:10

Friday night was the first funeral of the two. Jack's would be on Friday night and LaMar's on Saturday. How would I manage both? For Pete's sake, always thinking of myself—how would the congregation manage both? I am glad that our people, including me, expected a funeral to be a celebration of the life of the loved person who had left to live forever with the Savior. Especially when the person was…a senior…and the remembrance was delightfully happy, full of joy. The people of the congregation helped the family to laugh and feel the joy as they responded in unison to some favorite joke or story or even a sentimental picture or piece of lovely or uptempo music. I, for one, want "We need a little Christmas, right this very minute" to start out my funeral and Mark's. He agrees.

For every funeral we hold in the church, I arrive early and walk around the space, praying, asking God to bless the space and the participants and me, praying for my friend who has died, talking with the friend on the other side. When the funeral home folks arrive with the casket, I help with the set up. They know just what to do. They disappear, as they know my ways, and I sit with my friend and pray.

That Saturday afternoon when the friend was Jack, and I was praying, God gave me this to pray out-loud to my friend Jack.

Picture this, Jack. You find yourself in a dark wasteland. Look around; what do you see? The dark makes it difficult to see anything. You look for familiar markers—a tree, a house, another person— but you can't see anything you know. You strain to see into the far distance, but it's like being in an airplane at night, looking out the window into clouds. It's only dark. You can't seem to get a perspective on things. You know down because you feel something flat under you. You only know up because it's opposite from down. But how far up would you have to go to get to a star or the light from the moon? There's no left or right, east or west. You reach out and touch nothing.

How did you get here, Jack? You know it wasn't a good thing that got you here. It was some distress, some worry, some death, some happening that made it impossible for you to see the right way home. Name what got you here, Jack. (I waited for Jack to say, 'My death.') *What were you doing just before you got here? Were you looking for a friend, but no friend was around to be near you?* (Meaning I was sorry I was down the hall and not at your side, but it didn't matter now.) *Were you being attacked in some way, by someone, by self-doubt, by worry? Were you confused? Depressed?*

Stressed? Fearful? Lonely? (I took the words slowly as if Jack were to answer each one.)

How do you feel now? Are you still confused, fearful, worried, lonely, scared to death? (I foolishly laughed at my little joke. He'd appreciate it, I'm sure.)

You sit down and bring your knees up to your chest. Wrapping your arms around your legs, you hug your limbs to your heart. You assume the pre-natal position. (I know how comforting it is to be all tucked in to yourself.)

Then under the bottom of your feet, you feel warmth. It's not hot, more like someone holding hands with your feet. Just the bottoms are warm to the touch of the ground. It feels good. The warmth feels good, and being aware of another warmth feels good. You touch the ground with the palms of your hands and feel the warmth. You feel the warmth coming up from where you are sitting. You uncurl, stretch your legs out, and feel the warmth. You lean back and stretch out, and the warmth underlies your whole body. You roll over onto your stomach and press your belly and your cheek against the warmth, so glad you have found it.

Some of the darkness seems to have dissipated. You can see light, Jack, like looking into a cloud, but you can't see objects. You focus your eyes to see your own hand in front of your face. Then you look out and refocus your eyes to see far away. You look up and see changes in the clouds. At a far distance you begin to see a face—a huge face, like a giant a long way away.

You shout, "What are you? Are you a giant?" The face moves side to side as if it is saying no.

You shout, "Who are you?"

The answer comes gently, "I am."

"Yes?" you say, "Who are you?"

"I am the I am."

"God? You are God?"

"Yes, I am your God. Be not dismayed for I am your God. Fear not for I am with you."

"God, where am I? I am surrounded by nothingness."

"No, child, you are surrounded by me. It is my hand you are sitting on. (My own words, but I cry.) *It is the warmth of my hand that is warming your body. When you could see nothing else, you were in my hand. I am holding you. You are in the hand of your God. Now that you can see my face and hear my voice, you know that I am your God. I was always with you. When you could neither see nor feel anything or anyone, you were still in my hand. And when you open your eyes, and go into what you have called heaven, you will still be in my hand. For I am your God. I will always uphold you with my strong right hand."*

That's what the Holy Spirit said to me and what I said to Jack over the space between heaven and earth. I learned a lot from those words, and the words comforted me.

As a beloved minister of mine, Pastor Karena, used to say after she read a story from the Bible: "I don't know if it really happened that way, but I know it is the truth." Perhaps it's just another metaphor that the Holy Spirit gave me. It would probably not work from the pulpit, but I know the metaphor is the truth.

I come to know different answers from Jesus through the Holy Spirit. One day one answer works better than another, and cumulatively the answers work best as a whole. It might have something to do with spiritual maturity. I hope so.

They say that sometimes when a person is expected to die in a short period of time, like a day or two, and after a week they are still living, it may be a good idea for a loved one to give them permission to die. My father's kidneys gave up on him, and the doctor expected him to die within three days, but it didn't happen.

He was no longer talking, and he was only communicating through subtle changes in facial expressions which it didn't seem anyone but me could read. One time he was lying silently, and I was talking to him, and his brother walked through the door. I said, "Look who's here. It's Sam." And just like a thousand times before when his baby brother walked through the door, he extended his hand just a fraction to shake with Sam. I said to my Uncle Sam, "Look at that. He wants to shake hands with you."

Sam got a quizzical look on his face and said, "You're imagining things." Ah, we communicate in such subtle ways. I was saddened that Sam could not receive the very important gesture of greeting, especially in the Jewish family, just because it was illogical.

Later, when we were alone I talked to my father, and he gave subtle responses with his facial expressions. "Dad, are you ready to go to heaven? To meet God? I give you my permission. I know you don't need my permission, but just in case you may be thinking that you should stay around for my benefit, to take care of me like you've always done, I want to tell you that it's ok. I'll be alright on my own. I'm old enough now. Won't it be wonderful to see Mom again? Kiss her for me. And to see your Mother, too. There will be a huge party. All the deli food in heaven. Sounds great, huh. Are you ready? I'm ready. Any time now. I love you. Always remember that—I love you." He left for forever soon thereafter.

SIX

FEAR

The Protector God

*"Be strong and courageous. Do not be afraid...because
of them; for the Lord your God goes with you. He will
never leave you nor forsake you."* Deuteronomy 31:6

It felt good to go from two funerals on Friday and Saturday to
Children's Sunday School before the service the next Sunday
morning. Josie was a terrific teacher for a class of about fifteen
five year olds. She loved to tease the kids, not in a mean way but
supportively. And she knew the kids were growing up when they
started to tease her back. It's a grand moment, isn't it, when your own
kid sees something funny about what you said or did and passes it
back to you as a joke. I remember an in-joke that my Dad and I had
when I was in school. When I said that something was "weird" (a
favorite slang term I used often in high school, jargon of the day),
he would say back "eerie" in a spooky voice, and we'd both laugh
and say "eerie" about ten times between us while we laughed. Now

what's funny about that? Nothing. Mostly it just meant to me that he was listening, not a skill most fathers of the day were thought to have. I think teenagers underrated their fathers. Do they still do that? As I was giggling while I watched Josie and the kids in their Sunday School class, this went through the back of my mind. It was a whole story I had never heard before. I was making it up as it went along. I wrote it down in a fast minute in my office before the service. I hope it will make sense to you.

You picture a child. You know the child is you. How do you know? What do you look like? You, the child, is in a parking garage at the mall—by yourself. The lot is brightly lit. There are lots of cars and lots of people, too, all kinds of people—kids, parents, an old lady, a man walking a dog, a policeman. You smile as people pass you by, laughing, joking, talking to each other, eating chocolate ice cream cones. A lovely picture in your mind. An idyllic situation. The policeman says hi and tousles your hair as he walks past you. You watch him turn the corner.

Just as he is gone, the lights go out. It's almost dark. There is just enough light coming in from the parking level above that you can see the outline of the parked cars. It's quiet, too. All the cars have stopped moving, and there aren't any people that you can see. The policeman is nowhere to be seen either.

This is getting scary. What's happening? You speculate. What do you think might have happened?

The doors of the mall that used to have people coming in and out are dark. You're not even sure which direction they are. Then you hear the door open. You turn toward the noise, expectantly, hoping it's someone you know. But you don't see anybody. You hear a car door open...and close. It echoes. You can't tell where the car is. You call out, "Is somebody there?" No answer. You're getting really scared.

Then you hear the growl of a dog. You can't tell how close it is. You're very frightened. You call out, "If somebody's there, will you help me?"

Somebody behind you says quietly, "I'm here." You jump out of your skin and whirl around.

"Who's there?" you holler.

"It's me," he says as he lights a match, and then lights a candle. You can see him now, and you're relieved. It's Jesus. You're safe. "Don't be afraid," he says. "I'll stay with you until the lights come on." He takes you by the hand.

You see some people come out of the door of the mall with flashlights in their hand. It's a little boy and his mom. "Boy, it's dark out here," the little boy says to his mom.

"It's a good thing we have flashlights," his mom says. Jesus squeezes your hand, and the lights go on.

Maybe it's a story about kids who are afraid of the dark. Maybe it's for people who like scary movies. Not me. Maybe it's about LaMar and Jack, trying to find the way home. It's not a funny story for kids. I prefer funny stories.

SEVEN

FOR GROWTH, TO BECOME A NEW CREATION, MAKING CHANGE, FOR TRANSFORMATION

You Are the Pot

"Does not the potter have the right to make out of the same lump of clay some pottery for noble purposes and some for common use?" Romans 9:21

On the next Sunday a new-to-me family came to worship service with their two little kids, a girl about six and a boy ten. The odd thing, maybe unique is a better word, the Mom and Dad were basic white American, and the kids were maybe Columbian or from that part of the world. The first time I saw them I thought "war". That turned out to be a good guess. They were orphans, maybe brother and sister, found in the street. I say maybe because word going around was that they had been found together on the street when she

31

was a baby and he was four. He was begging and saying he needed food for his sister. I remember from a trip I took to Mexico when I was in college that the beggars would hold a child who had broken legs and couldn't walk, and the word was that the parent had broken its legs at birth so people would see the child and have pity and give them more money. A terrible thought.

The little girl was not handicapped. The two of them had been taken off the street to an orphanage. And the boy had insisted he stay with the girl as her brother until he had an offer from a couple from the United States for the two of them. Smart lad. He was gentle and kind to her, made her laugh, and nobody could push her around. That all sounds good—new parents, smart kid, sweet child. But there is more to the story. For one, he was a thief—a sociopath who had no trouble stealing, hurting others when cornered or just anytime for a reason or for no reason—including his parents but never his sister. He would yell and scream at home, run and hit, slam against the walls until it looked like he was hurting himself but never cry.

The parents came to see me for help. They had already been to the adoption people and their psychologists who encouraged patience and sending him to a special place, meaning away from home, in hopes to curb the bad behavior and encourage good. It actually worked for a short period of time. Then he reverted back, and the parents were sad and frightened and knew I could tell them how God fit into all of this. Oh boy. I prayed with them and told them to come back tomorrow.

In the meantime I prayed, and God gave me this, that I wrote down and then gave to them, quietly in my office.

Picture this. There you are—in the center of the potter's wheel— looking like an unformed lump of clay. You are spinning and spinning. and the world is turning around you. (They were nodding their heads already, so I knew they were catching it. Not everyone does.) *You're not frightened, or dizzy, or confused—because the strong hands of the potter are around you, forming you, pouring living water over you, turning you out.*

He gently takes his hands away and turns off the wheel. There you are. You are finished. You look exactly how you look today—formed by the potter. You know who the potter is. Who is it? Name the potter. (They both said it out loud.) *It is God. God looks at you and says, "It is good," just as God said when God created the world.*

God takes you gently in his hands and puts you on the shelf, along with all the other pots, where you dry. You feel pretty delicate now, like green ware.

Later God comes back and picks you up carefully, so you won't break. God puts you in the kiln where it's very hot, but you don't mind. The heat makes you strong; now you won't break so easily. When the kiln cools down, the potter comes back to take you out and put you back on a shelf. You like being there with all the other pottery—pots, vessels, dishes, bottles, some decorative and pretty, some practical and useful. You look pretty good among them. You hold your own. There's a lot of interaction that takes place among you, among the potter's pots. Some of it makes you happy, even joyful. Some makes you sad, some angry, some depressed.

Then it happens. You don't even see it coming. Whamo. You get hit by a hammer. Name the hammer. (Here they said the boy's name very quickly.) *Is it a person? Is it a happening? Is it a sadness? Is it a disaster?* (The father said, "A disaster is right." That was the first time I had smiled at the situation. Amen.)

You, the pot, are cracked. You have a big hole in your pottery. You don't get it. You were holding your own. You were doing alright. Then Wham. Smashed.

Whoa...pain. This really hurts.

Pieces of you begin to break away and fall off you. Pieces of your dirt and clay crumble. Will you be destroyed? Many others gather around you and take pieces away. So many people want a piece of you, you think you will disappear.

But look. Underneath the pieces that fall away are other pieces. Brightly colored, well formed. There is pain, but something else is being released. A new vessel. What does it look like? (They are quiet.)

The potter is there with you. You see the potter. The potter says, "It is good." And you know it is good.

What we did together that day in my office did not change the boy. Other smarter, more knowledgeable psychiatrists would do that. But it did change the parents. It began with a deep breath out,

In my mind's eye I can see myself in a hospital bed. I am just waking up from the anesthesia. I am so groggy that the room seems to have a sunny fog in it. I don't move; I only open my eyes. With my cheek on a pillow, what I see is a picture on its side. Straight ahead of me, my eyes focus on a gray-haired woman with her knitting on her lap and her chin on her chest—dozing. A little sound comes out of my throat that says, "I think I'm awake."

The little woman lifts her sleepy eyes and smiles at me. "So, you're awake," she says just above a whisper. "Everything's fine," she says. "Everything went just fine. You're going to be fine." She touches my cheek and strokes it. She touches my hair and strokes it. I believe her. She has never lied to me. I fall back to sleep.

In my mind's eye I see myself, curled up on my couch. There is a big, fluffy pillow under my head, and a soft blanket is tucked in around me as if my own mother tucked me in as the stars came out. Why am I curled up on the couch? Does something hurt? Some part of my body? Does my heart hurt? Does my soul hurt? My eyes are closed, and sometimes I take a big, deep breath to calm myself and send more healing oxygen to wherever it hurts.

Someone comes to me. With my eyes closed, I can't see who it is. Whom do I think it might be? Whom do I expect? The person strokes my cheek lightly to tell me, "I am here." The touch on my cheek is light and kind and gentle—just the stroke I needed. The person asks no questions, doesn't offer me Kleenex or chicken soup. The fingertips only stroke my cheek and my hair. I know I am not alone.

Who is this, so kind to be with me when I hurt? I open my eyes, and I'm surprised. It's Jesus. Jesus strokes my hair like a mother.

I remember the Psalm that says, "My soul finds rest in God alone."

In my mind's eye, I see myself leaning over a couch. The person on the couch is wrapped up in a blanket, head on a fluffy pillow. Occasionally the person takes a big, deep breath. I don't think the person is asleep. I see a hand wipe away a tear, and the muscles of the face frown, even though the eyes are closed. I reach down and stroke the person's cheek. I touch the hair. I want the person to know I am there.

I want to tell you a story about my Aunt Millie, but everything about her is coming to me only in snippets. I remember when I was sitting by Dad's deathbed, she didn't ask if she could come to be with me. She just came. And when I got the phone call from the hospital that he had died overnight, she said that now the pressure would be released, and I would be able to go traveling. She made me laugh. Aunt Millie was very practical.

When her youngest grandkid graduated from high school, he brought her a huge, empty glass jar for saving her coins with a sign on it that said, "For My Favorite Grandchild's College Education," and she thought it was the funniest thing ever. There was an inch of coins in it the first day. Aunt Millie was a very generous person.

While I was in college, she would give me a dress as a hand-me-down from last season, every season. It was usually my only new dress. Aunt Millie was stylish, and it was her own style.

She would take me to lunch at her club or at her favorite outdoor restaurant where the boats moor in Manhattan Beach. She lived in a "little tin house by the beach", that is, an adorable mobile home on the east side of Pacific Coast Highway at Huntington Beach. Aunt Millie was as adorable as her house by the ocean.

She would steal her neighbors' flowers on her walks around the neighborhood, claiming that it wasn't stealing because her neighbors knew she loved them and planted more just for her. Aunt Mille made me laugh.

At 85 she refused to wear comfortable running shoes because they weren't beautiful. Aunt Millie had an impeccable self-image.

For many of her elderly years I gave her the only thing she'd let me give her—chocolates with cashews and caramel. The candy for her birthday (that she pronounced bert'day) that she liked best was the batch I made myself. But See's candy came in second. Aunt Mille loved her some sweets.

When I was in college, I got extremely ill, and without missing a beat, she came after me in the dorms, took me into her house and nursed me back to health. Aunt Millie was a loving person.

She and her family had a wonderful log cabin in the mountains that they shared with family and friends. Mom and Dad and I spent every summer vacation with them there. In her family there were grown children and their little kids. I was in-between. I got very bored babysitting, and many a day she would stop doing what she liked to do and pump the player piano for me while we sang. Aunt Millie was a jewel.

She often reminded me that she and my mom used to sing on the radio when they were teenagers. Aunt Millie was also musical.

I finally got to do something for her. When I was a commercial producer/writer/director at the network station, I asked her to be in a commercial for a favorite client of mine, and we could use her living room. It was for the first emergency push button that seniors could wear. The script said she should grab her heart, push the button, and then fall down. She was perfect on the first take, but she popped back up and asked if we could do it again. Another time she was doing a commercial for me that had an old refrigerator in it. She was supposed to have trouble opening the door. For the first take she pulled so hard that the whole door came off. She let it fall and then turned to the camera and said...an inappropriate word. Needless to say we cut the audio, but if you watch very closely you can see her lips move. She was the hit of the studio. That was my Aunt Millie. Aunt Millie was a gas.

NINE

FOR PROTECTION

The Armor of God

"Therefore put on the full armor of God, so that when the day of evil comes, you may be able to stand your ground ...Stand firm then, with the belt of truth buckled around your waist, with the breastplate of righteousness in place, and with your feet fitted with the readiness that comes from the gospel of peace...Take up the shield of faith, with which you can distinguish all the flaming arrows of the evil one. Take the helmet of salvation, and the sword of the Spirit, which is the word of God."
Ephesians 6:13-17

"The Angel of the Lord encamps around those who fear him, and he delivers them." Psalm 34:7

There's nothing like a bunch of fourth graders for being smart, creative, and blowing the pastor's mind. My kids are so witty, so insightful. Once I asked them to draw God. They all seemed to know what they should draw. Some drew an old white dude with a long white robe and a long white beard. Those two were attending Catholic School. Some drew the sky with cloud formations and stars. Maybe that was as far up as they could see. Some drew pictures of nature, a tree with a pond, some birds in flight. Those kids lived in the country surrounding the town and raised dogs. I found them fascinating.

The best one-liner a kid in the fourth grade ever gave me came the day we were studying the Lord's Prayer, and I asked them what it meant to pray "Give us this day our daily bread." She said that daily bread meant our food that we ate every day, but then she stopped herself with "No! No! No! It means, you know how the bread on Sunday means Jesus' body. Well, it means give us this day our daily Jesus. We want to have Jesus with us every day." A fourth grade theologian came up with that gem.

They loved to hear stories from me. Sometimes I would tell them stories from the Bible. Sometimes I would make up some parable that would teach a lesson like Jesus did. Here's one that kept their attention and even made them bug out their eyes—great reactions.

Come with me, will you? I'm going to take you into a forest. Picture you and me alone together as we walk down the garden path toward the forest. The path is pretty, edged by wildflowers, and the sun is shining on a gentle spring day. All is well in God's world. We are healthy, and we walk with a sprightly gait.

Everything is pleasant here. Somehow it reminds you of Eden—perfection. A baby deer nibbles on some tender leaves of a bush. Her mother watches over her, watching us carefully, but she somehow knows that we are not going to hurt her fawn.

All of a sudden we spot a huge bear lumbering toward us. He stops as if to say, "Did you bring my dinner?" We're glad he doesn't mean, *"Are you my dinner?"* *I could swear he smiles at us before he turns and lumbers away.*

We look at each other, and relieved, we laugh.

We hear a rumble of thunder far away. "What's that?" you say. It's just thunder, and it's a long way away. But then the rumble sounds again—and it's not a long way off. It's right under our feet. The ground shakes like an earthquake. It's a frightening sound, and the rolling ground sends us to our knees. The earth shakes again, the sky darkens, and the boom of the thunder comes in even rolls toward us like the footsteps of a storybook giant.

The sky lights up in bright bursts of lightening—no, not lightening but bursts of flame like a mystical dragon in a storybook. The pages of the storybook open before us with real creatures and movie special effects.

But Deus Ex Machina, Jesus is there to protect you. "Quick!" Jesus says, "Put on the armor of God. The day of evil has come. You must be able to stand your ground."

You take the armor from Jesus and quickly strap it on. "Stand firm then," Jesus tells you. "Buckle the belt of truth around your waist. Here, put on the breastplate of righteousness. Put these wings on your feet. Your feet are fit with readiness. Dressed like that you are protected from the evil one."

The mystical dragon blows smoke in our faces and hurls rocks at us. I am so frightened, but you are strong, and you protect me.

"Take up the shield of faith," Jesus tells you, "so you can fend off the evil one. Take the helmet of salvation and the sword of the Spirit which is the word of God."

With your sword at the ready, you stand firm protecting yourself and protecting me. You are a standard bearer of the gospel of peace.

The mystical dragon sees you and knows you are a formidable foe. You raise your sword above your head ready to strike, but there is no need to strike. The evil one recognizes you as a child of God, protected by Jesus and his righteousness. He turns and runs away, wailing because he has lost in a confrontation with you.

And now, picture this. You stand with me and Jesus, and you see the helmet and shield you are wearing as they melt. But they don't melt away. They melt...into your skin. They become a part of you.

The steel of the sword strengthens your backbone. The wings on your feet wrap themselves around your legs and become a part of your body. The standard you hold that made you a standard bearer of the gospel of peace becomes a Bible in your hand.

You feel strong now, capable of fending off any foe with your strong backbone and your protected body. You are a child of God, protected by God. You walk through the darkened forest and feel calm.

In a few moments the sun breaks through the darkening clouds, and we can see around us again. Everything has returned to the way it was. But you are not the same. You walk taller now.

What an amazing reaction I got. Of course I was amazing in my theatrical rendition, but they were the best audience ever. And the best part is that it's straight from the Bible—well, almost straight.

TEN

FOR KNOWING GIFTS

How Am I Gifted?

"There are different kinds of gifts but the same Spirit;
there are different kinds of service but the same Lord!"
Corinthians 12:4-5

I can't resist telling you stories about my fourth graders. It was nearly Christmas. We had put up a Christmas tree. They had decorated it with the Christian symbols—Chrismons—and surrounded it with gifts for the poor families that live in temporary housing locally. I wrote a script about gifts and talked my way through it so it sounded something like this.

We have a tall and beautiful Christmas tree. It is decorated more extravagantly than any Christmas tree we have ever had here in the church. It is as big as the Rockefeller Square tree in New York—well, almost—with lights that twinkle and ornaments galore. Beautiful ornaments, too, all symbols of Jesus Christ: lambs, fish, Greek letters of Alpha and Omega, stars, kingly crowns, crosses, roses, vines with grapes, suns—anything you can think of that represents our Lord Jesus Christ called Chrismons.

The tree is surrounded by gifts—presents wrapped in the fanciest wrapping topped by elegant ribbons. Anyone would want all these gifts. You don't even know what is in each of these gift boxes yet, but already you know you want them—for yourself, for your family, for your friends. You know they are not all for you. You would be willing to share, wouldn't you?

Now picture this. You see a mass of people around you. There's your family. There are your closest friends. Here are people from your neighborhood and your school, and here are people from your church. My goodness, everyone is here that you ever have contact with. Even some people who you only know by name, but you've never met. What is this all about?

You'll find out now. Somebody is calling for your attention. It seems to be a leader of some kind. Maybe it's the host of the program. Oh, you see who it is now—it's Jesus. Jesus calls everybody together. He says he has gifts for everybody—at least one gift for everybody, for some lots of gifts. He says that the gifts aren't based on your need, but rather they are based on his need. How odd?

You wonder what is in these packages. Then he begins to call out people by name, and to each person he gives a gift. To some he gives lots of gifts. Every person gets something. No one is missed.

Then he calls your name. You respond immediately. You are very excited, but you don't want to appear too greedy. He hands you several gift boxes.

Then you hear him tell everybody you know to open their gifts. And he says that everybody should call out what their gifts are. How exciting, you say. And this is what you hear:

I have the message of wisdom.

My gift is faith.

Jesus gave me the gift of prophecy.

There are two gifts here that are tied together—tongues and the interpretation of tongues.

I'm given a talent for music.

My gift is with numbers.

Mine is with languages.

My wife's gift is leadership.

My husband's is with children.

My gift is for generosity and good stewardship.

My friend the doctor has the gift of healing.

I'm not a doctor, and I got the gift of healing, too.

My gift is teaching.

Mine is teaching, too, and look, I got a Bible, too.

You listen for the longest time as everybody you know names the gifts Jesus gave them. What do you hear?

What gifts do the people in your family receive?

What gifts does your best friend receive from Jesus?

Then you hear Jesus say, "I've given each of you gifts, some one gift, some many. It doesn't matter how many you get. These are the gifts I need you to have. That may be a surprise to you. Right this minute you may not know what to do with these gifts. That will come. As you pray and ask me, I will show you. Later, as I need you to have other gifts, I will give them to you. These are practical gifts. I don't give perfume and ties. Use these gifts for the building up of the Kingdom."

You've watched as everybody you know has received their gifts, opened them, shouted out what gifts they were given. You listened as Jesus told you to use them. But you haven't opened your gifts yet. Jesus smiles at you. "Open your gifts," Jesus says to you. You excitedly unwrap the first. There they are—your gifts. (In each box is a tag saying what gift the person is receiving.) *What do you see?*

Shout out what your gifts are.
Is it what you expected? More than you expected? When much
is given, much is expected.
How will you use these gifts?
How will you help to build up the Kingdom?

Then the talking came. The kids fell easily into the game. Where one had trouble figuring out what the gift was, some other kid helped him out. I hardly talked at all. I had used what I knew about each kid to come up with a gift that they could relate to. It was a fascinating discussion. They all learned so much. At the end I asked them what they thought were the gifts Jesus wanted me to have for him. What an eye opener. Love surrounded me. Pint size love.

ELEVEN

For Belonging to God, Following Jesus

Bicycle Built for Two

"Teacher, I will follow you wherever you go." Matthew 8:19

"My sheep listen to my voice; I know them, and they follow me." John 10:27

"You do not belong to the world, but I have chosen you out of the world." John 15:19

"You are among those who are called to belong to Jesus Christ." Romans 1:6

I was teaching Youth Group. A tough audience. I knew I had to be a little over the top for them to stay with me, so I came up with this crazy script. I had them act it out as I read the script. I cast them first and dressed them in the costume of the characters. Here goes.

*Picture yourself on the **"Which is the Real Jesus?" Game Show.***

Behind Door #1 is Jesus as a judge. See the long white beard and the black judge's robe? This Jesus keeps track of the things you do wrong. He judges whether you deserve heaven or hell when you die.

Behind Door #2 is a picture of Jesus in a business suit. It's not him; it's just a picture of him. He's the President of the company, the Big CEO in the Sky. You recognize him, but you don't really know him.

Behind Door #3 is Jesus on the back seat of a tandem bike, a bicycle built for two. The front seat is empty and waiting for you. If you get on, Jesus will always be in back keeping you stable and providing the power that helps you pedal along the winding road of life.

Which door do you choose? Door #1: Jesus as judge? Door #2: Jesus as CEO? Door #3: Jesus as cyclist? Picture yourself choosing the door. What kind of response do you get from Jesus when you choose the door?

Let's say you choose Door #3: Jesus as cyclist. Picture yourself as you walk over to Jesus who is on this bicycle built for two. Jesus says to you, "I'm glad you chose me. I've been hoping and praying that you would. I've been waiting a long time. Get on." So you take the front seat.

"Where shall we go?" Jesus says. *"You have the handlebars up front, so you get to decide and take us wherever you want us to go. My job is to be the power behind you and just pedal for all I'm worth. And I can tell you, I'm one mighty strong pedal-er."*

"Let's go!" you say, and you take off across the flat.

"Where are we going?" Jesus asks as he pedals with his powerful legs.

"You don't get to ask that, Jesus. I'm in charge of the handlebars. I'm the one in control." And you pedal, and Jesus pedals, and you cycle across the flat together. You go, and you go, and you go some more—straight ahead full speed.

You're starting to get bored. This flat you're pedaling on is a little dull.

Out there in the middle of the flat is a rock. By accident you hit it. The bicycle flies up, and you and Jesus go head over heels. You crash. You've got a skinned knee and a busted pride.

Then Jesus says, *"Would you like me to take a turn up front? It would mean you would have to give up control. I'd have the handlebars instead of you."* You think for a minute and rub your hurting knee.

You say, *"Let's give it a try,"* and you get back on the bike, this time on the rear seat.

And that's when the action begins. All of a sudden the boring flat turns into a mountain road. Tall pines flank each side as the road wiggles up and down mountains. You hang on for all you're worth. This is one exciting ride—what an adventure!

Then the scenery changes, and you're pedaling along a seashore, right out on the edge of the cliffs. You see crashing waves below, and the spray slaps your face. You call to Jesus, *"Jesus, I'm scared!"* Jesus leans back and holds your hand. *"Hold on to me. I'll keep you safe."*

What a journey he takes you on. Busy city streets—the center of the action. Wide pastoral views that warm your heart with their beauty. Sometimes you get scared with being in all the new and different places, but Jesus just tells you to hold on--he's in charge.

It's amazing what he knows about that bike. You take sharp corners like you're in a race. You fly through streams. You stop on a dime when something gets in your way that needs Jesus' attention.

"This is the life, Jesus!" you say. "I love the adventure when you're in change."

He just smiles and says, "Pedal!"

Luckily a family in the church had a two-seater bicycle and a stand that held it, so they could pedal and go nowhere. They got excited with the script and started yelling instructions to the cyclists. My girls were the ring leaders, of course. They even created a race and did the play by play of the sports announcer. They laughed. And they got it. When we talked about what the metaphor meant, they understood the difference between the back seat and the front seat and giving up control, and they came up with examples of what that could mean and then experiences in their own life. What fun I had. What fun they had. I'm still grinning.

TWELVE

ANGER

The Weight on Your Shoulders

"Father, forgive them, for they know not what they are doing." Luke 23:34

If I could get days with the kids for an hour every day, I'd be happy, but the life of a pastor is more complex. I do a lot of one-on-one counseling and family counseling. Most of the counseling is around one of about ten themes. Here's a big one—forgiveness—and it usually comes in the form of anger.

I was at the church. Two of the senior women of the church came in to see me one day. I knew one fairly well after I had been about two months at the church. Her husband had died unexpectedly, and I had done the funeral. I liked what I knew about her. She and her husband had invited me to dinner my first week and were gentle and delighted that I was happy at their home and at the church. About three weeks later they took me to the restaurant that served ethnic food of their nationality. Mostly they told stories, which is great for a new pastor.

I didn't know the second one much. She was sort of a sidekick of a more outgoing woman of the same age, and I didn't hear much from her unless it was to agree with a complaint that the leader of the pack was voicing. The two women sat at opposite sides of the pastor's office. I noted that we formed a triangle, which was more common with an arguing husband and wife.

The leader spoke. The widow did not. The problem was the first I had heard such a one—ever. I was to stop doing this. It seems in preparation for decorating the church for Christmas, I had given an announcement in church inviting just anyone to come at a particular time to decorate the church. Just everyone was not invited, she told me. We already had our same committee of people who did it every year; they knew how to do it; we didn't want anyone new to come and mess things up. Note that I had already "messed things up" by offering design suggestions when they had told me previously that no one wanted to be in charge. Oh my, thought I. What to say? What to do? I told them, with restraint, that it sounded to me like we were cutting people out of participating in the church, and our church professed to welcome everyone. No response. Noses lifted a little higher. Really. I said, Perhaps we can compromise. What if I were to say I would not give another announcement to invite everyone, but you would graciously accept and welcome anyone who came. The response, "We knew you wouldn't do what we wanted."

I turned to the woman I knew and said, "What are you thinking? What do you think I should do?"

She said nothing.

I commented…softly, "You seem very upset. Is this what's upsetting you or something else?"

After an uncomfortable pause and a couple of snorts from the other woman (really!), she said, "I'm considering leaving the church."

I pulled back. She had giving me as good a welcome as anyone outside of the search committee.

"Will you tell me why?"

"No." Another wait. "It takes me a long time to think something through before I do something about it."

"I'd be happy to help you think it through. We could work on it together, if you'd like."

"I wouldn't like. I'll let you know what I decide. Better, you'll know if I'm here or not."

"My door is always open. To both of you." They left, the leader making as much noise as possible, sliding chairs, coughing, slamming doors. The silence reverberated.

I felt like laughing and crying at the same time. I wanted desperately to tell somebody, but that's a no-no in the congregation. I needed to think it thorough before I decided to share with the Area Minister, whom I admired. As it happened, I waited to share the story until I had half a dozen of like ones from a handful of the same people. The Area Minister had trouble not laughing. I finally laughed aloud, which relaxed him and gave him the safe space to agree with me. But, oh dear, this was to be a short ministry.

Forgiveness. Notwithstanding the laughter and considering repeat performances of that small group, I had a mountain to forgive. I had help from the Search Committee and the Pastor that took the pulpit when I left and the Area Minister and from several church people who were gentle, good people and could see the truth through the mud and supported me. All that was good, but I still had a devil of a time feeling forgiveness to those who had been so cruel to me. It's done now, partially because of this imagery conjured up for me by the Holy Spirit. When an idea, images like this, comes, I know it isn't my own work but God working through the way that my mind works. Here it is. Consider that the one talking to me is the Holy Spirit.

Picture yourself standing at the bottom of a staircase. It's a staircase you take every day to reach a place you need to go to every day. Other days, it's easy for you to climb. Remember the day you climbed it comfortably in about ten seconds. Picture yourself in the past climbing the stairs in ten seconds.

But today is different. Today you have a terrible, huge weight on your shoulders. Feel the weight on your shoulders. Try to climb the first step. You aren't able to because there is such a weight on your shoulders.

The weight is a person you are angry at. Name that person. That person has the whole weight of his body on your shoulders, holding you down. You can barely stand up under the weight, let alone climb a stair.

What caused you to be so angry at this person? Did she hurt you? Did he offend you or do something thoughtless? Was she mean to you or worse? Was he more interested in himself or someone else than he was in making relationship with you? As you think about why you are angry at this person, you feel the anger—in your shoulders, in your head, in your stomach, in your lower back. Each time you think of a body part while you are angry at this person, that body part reacts. Try it. Think of your shoulders where that person is lying on your shoulders. Now think of the muscles in your neck that tighten and ache when you think of the person. Now feel the headache in your temples as they pulse with your anger. Now your stomach aches; it feels queasy, a little nauseous—all because you think of that person. You're a mess of pain, and frustration, and anger.

You see someone coming toward you. You are afraid it's the person you are angry with, and your body tightens. Every muscle tenses. You try to hide, but there's nothing to hide behind. But wait. It isn't that *person. Who is it? Well, look, it's Jesus. What joy that brings you! Jesus is here!*

You say to Jesus, "Jesus, why are you here? I didn't call you."

Jesus says quietly to you, "No, you didn't call me. You didn't pray. I came anyway. I know that you need me. I'm the only one who can help you."

You say, "How can you help me?"

Jesus says, "I can help you get that weight off your shoulders."

"Great," you say. "Get this person off my shoulders!"

"Oh, I can't do that," Jesus says. "You can do that yourself."

"No, I can't. I've been trying all day. I keep reaching up to pull

him off, and he escapes me. I yell at her. I even tried hitting him with a stick, and I missed and hit my head."

"But that's not the way," Jesus says. "Remember what I told you."

You answer, "Who can forgive sins but God alone."

"Oh no, that wasn't me. That was the Pharisees, and you know how they got it all messed up. No, I told you to turn the other cheek. I told you to forgive no matter who did what to you. Not only did I forgive the thieves nailed on crosses next to me, I also forgave the Roman soldiers who nailed me to the cross, and the people who yelled for Barabbas, and Pilate who washed his hands of me. I forgave them all. They put the cross on my back that I pulled through the streets to Golgotha. Is the person on your shoulders heavier than the cross I pulled and hung on?"

"No, Jesus," you answer. "Nothing is heavier than your cross."

"Then what must you do with the weight on your shoulders?"

You know the answer.

In the midst of unspeakable death in South Carolina when a gunman murdered eight people and their Pastor in a Bible Study at an AME Church, President Barack Obama gave the eulogy at the funeral for Reverend Pinckney. President Obama said that the Reverend Pinckney knew the power of grace and forgave the stranger-killer, that he received grace with gratitude, a free and benevolent gift of God. And the President followed that with a heartfelt rendition of "Amazing Grace" that brought the congregation to their feet and tears to my eyes.

THIRTEEN

For Receiving forgiveness

Take It--It's Yours

*"For if you forgive men when they sin against you, your
Heavenly Father will also forgive you."* Matthew 6:14

"Forgive and you will be forgiven." Luke 6:37

Many, many years ago, some thirty years ago, I said something small
that was unintentionally mean and nasty that I didn't even mean to
someone I loved very much, and it ruined our close relationship. I
thought I had apologized and that he had forgiven me on the spot.
I was wrong. Time and distance separated us, and when I made
contact again, I found out that he had not forgiven me, and it broke
my heart. He died, and my heart is still broken that it is too late to
be forgiven except by God but not by my friend.

Years ago, steeped in that pain, I wrote this dialogue between
me and Jesus. I knew what I was saying was true at the time I said
it, but I put it away and didn't find it again until I was writing this
book. In that time I must have forgotten the message of forgiveness,

and I've suffered many times feeling that I had not been forgiven by God and my friend. I look forward to the hereafter when I can ask him for his forgiveness face to face and renew our friendship. As in the last dialogue, the Holy Spirit and Jesus are speaking to me.

Picture this. You are sitting in a corner, your feet curled up under you, your back to the wall. You have been crying. You have been crying about something you have done wrong. Why have you been crying?

You feel very alone. And in your loneliness and depression, Jesus comes to you. With your eyes closed, you hear him call your name. He says to you, "Open your eyes and see me."

"No, I can't," you say. "I don't deserve to be in your presence. I don't deserve to see you."

Jesus answers, "Yes, you do. I tell you that you do. I will always come to you, and you can always be with me."

"No, Jesus. You don't know what I've done."

"Yes, I do. I've come to forgive you. Even though you didn't ask me to come to forgive, I've come. Now open your eyes. I want you to see my crown."

You say, "I know your crown. The crown of thorns the soldiers put on your head before they crucified you. The crown of thorns meant to humiliate you. I deserve that crown of thorns."

"Open your eyes," Jesus says, "and see my crown."

You slowly open your eyes. You shrink back a bit because the brightness of the sun shines through the jewels on Jesus' crown. They shimmer in the light, and the gold reflects the brightness. "You see," says Jesus. "It is not a crown of thorns. It is the crown of a king. And today this crown represents your forgiveness. I want to give this crown to you as a symbol of your forgiveness."

"Is it heavy? I will wear it on my head as a symbol of my heavy sin."

"No, dear one. It is not heavy at all. Here let me put it on your head, and you will feel its lightness. It's incredible lightness."

Jesus takes the shimmering crown from his head and puts it on your head. You can see the glow as it lights your face, but you feel nothing. The crown has no weight at all.

"That's right," he says. "No weight at all. In fact it has lifted the weight of the sin that was weighing you down. It is the crown of forgiveness. I give it to you."

Like the leper who was cured and returned to Jesus, you thank him. "Thank you, Lord, for forgiving me."

"Next time you need forgiveness, and there will be a next time, remember this crown. Remember that to receive it, you need only to ask. I will bring you forgiveness whenever you ask. Don't punish yourself unnecessarily. Forgive yourself as I forgive you. Promise me."

"I promise," you say, and Jesus leaves, but you know that he will return whenever you ask.

The first time I read it out-loud to put it in the book, I choked on "Don't punish yourself unnecessarily." I felt ashamed and at the same time relieved. It was a truth I didn't remember until now. The shame was so vibrant that the glare of it blocked out the truth of forgiveness. Perhaps I should feel like dancing, but I am happy enough to sit here quietly in a corner, my feet curled up under me, my back to the wall. No more tears.

FOURTEEN

FOR FORGIVING OTHERS

The Big Bully

"If you forgive others their sins and faults, your Heavenly Father will also forgive you. But if you do not forgive others their sins and faults, neither will your Father forgive you." John 20:23

Another message on forgiveness, but note this one is backwards. It's about my responsibility to forgive someone else who asks for my forgiveness. Have you had that happen to you? You are mad as a wet hen at someone who says he or she is sorry for doing this nasty thing to you, and no way are you going to forgive him/her. It sounds very childish, doesn't it? Have you ever split up two kids on the playground and said automatically, "Now aren't you sorry you hit Bill?" Remember the courtroom lawyer's number one rule: "Never ask a question that you don't know the answer to." Is Johnny ever sorry he hit Billy? Have you ever tried to comfort your crying teenage daughter telling her to accept her basketball player boyfriend Shane's apology for breaking their date to the movies because the coach is making him go to practice? That's hopeless, too. Just stay out of it, and wait a couple years before she might understand this deep theological principle again that she knew when she was nine years old in Sunday School. The teenage mind is a sieve.

Here's an imaginative scene on the playground. I love playground stories. They sound so innocent, and they can be so thought provoking. Look for the word "Decision".

Picture yourself on the elementary school grounds ready to play. How old are you? Where's your best friend? Standing right by you? On the jungle bars? Hitting a fly ball over the wall? You watch your friend from a distance, proud of your friend's strength and ability and prowess on the playground.

As you watch, a very big sixth grader comes up to your friend and says something to him that makes him frown, and he turns away. But the sixth grader follows him, talking and then yelling at him and finally grabs his arm, swings him around and punches him in the stomach. You take off running toward the bully and your friend. You see your friend get up slowly, say something to the bully, and just as you get there, the bully pushes your friend from behind and your friend falls. What do you do?

Do you stand between them? Do you holler for the teacher? Do you hit the bully? Do you knock him to the ground and keep punching?

Now picture that your friend is Jesus. Jesus gets up now. He's on his feet. Just as you raise your fist in the air, Jesus grabs it, so you can't follow through. He says quietly to you, "That's all." He turns to the bully and says quietly to him, "That's all."

It's all over. The bully walks away. You walk away with Jesus. The fight may be over, but your anger is not. Jesus has turned the other cheek. But you have not. How dare that bully attack Jesus! How dare he!

Jesus tells you, "You must forgive him because he knows not what he does."

"But, Jesus," you say. "Not only does that mean bully insult you and hit you, but he hits YOU, the Son of God. How can we stand for that! I'm so angry!"

"Yes, you're angry. But anger is an emotion, and forgiving is a decision, not a feeling. If we waited until we felt like forgiving the other person, we wouldn't ever forgive anyone."

"But he doesn't deserve it!" you say.

"Forgiveness isn't based on the other person deserving it. That's judging him, being judgmental. The opposite of forgiving is judging. You must choose not to be judgmental but to forgive. You must make the decision to forgive."

"Why must I?" you ask Jesus.

Jesus sighs, as if to say, "How many times must I tell you this?!" and then he quietly tells you again, "Because if you do not forgive others their sins and faults, neither will your Father forgive you."

How do you answer Jesus? What do you say next?

Then Jesus smiles at you, reaches out with his hand and touches your heart, and then your head.

FIFTEEN

For Self-Acceptance

Self-image

The youth in the Youth group wanted to give a night of one act plays that they had written to each other. Each age group wanted to write a little play about something they had learned from Youth group. The little kids were expected to do comedy, but the oldest kids said they wanted to do something about their relationship with Jesus. Each of them shared with the others something personal about the relationship, and they had decided on self-image which seemed to be a topic repeated often among them, both boys and girls. That was not a surprise to me. I watched them all struggle with that one, even my cousin's son, Jake. It started out about seventh grade and peaked about tenth. He had come to terms with it about eleventh grade and then helped others of his friends with their struggle. It wasn't any easier for the boys than the girls in Youth group. Teachers and coaches were helpful, usually, except for one teacher they all had, who was destructive for them. Enough of that.

They wanted to write a little play about self image. They also wanted to include the Bible—and Jesus—and costumes, so said all the girls and none of the boys. All the girls wanted to be actors. So did a couple of boys. They wanted Jessica to be the head writer because she was terrific and had taken a playwriting class as a senior in which she aced every paper. Jessica promised her best friend a beautiful Biblical costume if she didn't force her to act. It was a deal. The others in the group introduced the characters, narrated (without memorization), directed, assistant directed, were lighting techs, sound techs, and took various tech positions, most of which were never seen on another stage. After they wrote a part for a younger child, the youngest girl was cast from the techies. Luckily she looked a lot like Jessica, which helped in their play.

NARRATOR: *(Youngest girl Anne enters, stands upstage of the empty frame of a full-body mirror facing the audience.)* Picture yourself as a child. You, the child, are standing in front of a mirror.

As you look into the mirror, you see your feet and legs. You see your body and your arms and your hands. You know your little body well. You look up and see your hair, so familiar to you. You look in the mirror expecting to see your face, but instead of eyes, nose and mouth, there is a blur. (*A piece of voile or silk has been placed over her face and glued on.*) You squint your eyes to see your face, but it doesn't come into focus. You know that this is an issue of self-acceptance. You know that if you accepted yourself as good, valuable and of worth, your face would come into focus.

Now you see two people coming toward you, hand in hand. *(Enter Suzanne and Jake)* You recognize Jesus. The second is a woman. You don't know her face. When they come to you, Jesus calls you by name and says to you,

JESUS: "This is Naomi. You know Naomi. You know her story in the book of the Bible named for her daughter-in-law Ruth. Tell her about yourself, Naomi."

NARRATOR: Naomi begins to tell her story to you.

NAOMI *(Suzanne, the oldest boy and another young woman and two young men follow):* "So many bad things had happened. My husband died. *(He walks away.)* My two sons died. *(They walk off.)* One of my daughters-in-law left us. *(Other girl walks off.)* I told her to. She needed to go back to her people who would care for her. There was no one left to care for us. Only Ruth stayed with me. She shouldn't have. It was very dangerous. She could have died. I was so bitter—I called myself Mara, which means bitter."

NARRATOR: Naomi doesn't frighten you even though the things she says are frightening. But she speaks in a gentle voice as if all of this bitterness was a long, long time ago. You see a tear run down Naomi's cheek, and Jesus puts his arm around her shoulder. Following Jesus, you *(Anne)* reach out and take Naomi's hand. She smiles a thank you for your kindness. Jesus tells her,

JESUS: "Go on, Naomi."

NAOMI: "We went to the land of my ancestors, hopefully in order to get help. I was not healthy. I was quite old, but Ruth was strong and healthy, and she walked out in the fields and picked up the bits and pieces of grain, *(workers gather stalks, leave some)* a few stalks that were left behind when the workers collected it. There was a tradition that anyone could have those leftovers. The law was to help the poor and hungry to get a little sustenance.

"There was another law that said our nearest relative could marry us if they wanted to. Well, the story gets complex here, but the end of the story is that Boaz, *(Boaz enters.)* who was our kinsman redeemer, saw Ruth and admired her—who wouldn't?--and fell in love with her and married her. And they had a child *(Ruth and all the cast come on.)* who was an ancestor of Jesus."

RUTH: "So you see, all that mara—bitterness—needed to happen so that I could be a grandmother many generations later to King David and many generations after that to this man here, Jesus, the Son of God."

JESUS: "God bless you, Grandmother Naomi, God bless you for your suffering and bitterness so that God could change your name again to Grandmother."

NARRATOR: Now Jesus turns to you.

JESUS: "Tell Naomi your name, child."

NARRATOR: What name do you tell her? Do you call yourself Mara? Or Lonely? Or Rejected? Or Nameless? What is your name? (*She tries to speak her name but cannot.*) Then Jesus continues to you,

Jesus: "God will change your name, child. Your name will no longer be lonely, rejected, nameless, Mara. Now you will be called by your real name as I am called Jesus. Say your real name to yourself. (*All the participants say their own name—then continue to repeat it over and over four times.*)

"Now name some other names. Name your ancestors. (*All the participants say the name of an ancestor*) Who are you named after? (*They all name the names.*)

"Name the names of women in your circle of empowerment. (*All do.*)

"Name your women ministers or women who minister to you. (*All do.*)

(*To one of the other girls*) "Do you know my mother's name?

(*To the other girl*) Yes, it is Mary.

JESUS: There are many Marys in the Bible. If many women had your name, what would be your middle name to differentiate you? Mary called Magdalene. Mary the Prostitute. The other Marys. Are you the other ones? Are you another Mary at the cross, another Mary in the house with the disciples, another Mary at the tomb?

"I will tell you your middle name. If your name is Mary, your name is Mary the Beloved. You are 'the Beloved.'"

"Say your name and follow it with "the Beloved".

The Girl: "Mary the Beloved"

Jesus: "You all say your name. *(They do.)* Say it again with 'the Beloved.' *(They do.* Then to the first little girl)* Now look into the mirror again. Now you can see your face *(Pulls off the gauze)*— your sparkling eyes, your full smile. That is because now you know you are the Beloved. Say your name again and follow it with 'the Beloved'." *(She does.)*

NARRATOR: You bless Naomi,

ALL: "Bless you, Naomi."

NARRATOR: And you bless Jesus for coming to you and giving you your name, the Beloved.

ALL: "Bless you, Jesus."

Narrator: Characters. *(Mirror)* Look again into the mirror. As your face comes into focus in the mirror, you know who you are. You are the Beloved.

(All the participants say their own name—then continue to repeat it over and over as they bow.)

They were a hit. All that creativity. All that youthful exuberance. The message. The Bible characters. The audience loved it. So did I. I think Jesus was pleased.

SIXTEEN

FOR FRIENDS, SUPPORT, TRUST

I Call You Friend

"I no longer call you servants, for a servant does not know his master's business. Instead I have called you my friends, for everything I have learned from my Father, I have made known to you." John 15:15

"Jesus wept." John 11:35

"Make new friends, but keep the old.
One is silver, but the other is gold." An American folk song

Their younger sisters and brothers told them they wanted to do a play like that.

A happy event came out of the heart-filled time with the oldest kids in youth group, but the message also came through that they didn't want to have to memorize any lines. So the now-famous playwright said she could write that. She would put the speakers

74

at the edge of the stage with mikes, and actors would mime, and she asked what they wanted the play to be about. They said friends. Perfect. They came to me excited, and I made a special day they could perform on Sunday. I asked who was going to be in it. They said all the kids and a few adults would be needed, too. (I only had to move the date back three times, but I went with the flow.) This was their script:

"Friends"

Littlest kids come out dressed as pink and purple flowers.

Enter the character named "YOU".

NARRATOR: Picture yourself in a field, pink and purple with wildflowers and warm with the spring sunshine. Who is that coming toward you? (*Enter Mary and Martha and Jesus.*) One man and two women. The man you know. It is Jesus, Savior and friend. But who are the women?

Sensing your confusion, Jesus calls you by name,

JESUS: Hello, YOU.

NARRATOR: and says,

JESUS: Let me introduce you to two women you know by reputation. This is Mary. This is Martha. They are sisters. Lazarus is their brother. Do you remember hearing about them?

YOU: Oh yes, you answer. Mary, you were at your home in Bethany with the disciples, and you sat at Jesus' feet and learned from him.

Martha, you are the sister who saw your call and your role as a woman in those days to cook and feed the disciples.

NARRATOR: Jesus says to you,

JESUS: Do you remember the day my friend Lazarus was raised from the dead?

YOU: I remember the story. Martha came out to meet you on the road to tell you her brother had died. She told you that she knew you were the Christ.

JESUS: That's right, and then she brought Mary to me. And we cried together. We cried because Lazarus, my friend, was dead. Three friends together, supporting and loving one another, full of grief. We shared a part of one heart.

YOU: Yes, three friends.

JESUS: I had so many friends when I was on earth. *(All twelve disciples enter.)* The disciples, of course: I taught them and trusted them with the gospel, the words of the Father, to be taught all over the world. *(Peter steps out.)* Peter...what a friend Peter was. He'd do anything for me. There were many extraordinary men who were friends with me, but the dearest of my friends were women. *(Women step out.)* Did you know that?

YOU: Women were the dearest to you?

JESUS: Yes, my mother Mary. *(Mary steps out with a little child.)* She lived her life to raise me to be ready for my ministry, and she never left me. (*Child steps back.*) Her heart was always with me, even in my last moments on earth.

YOU: And Mary Magdalene? She was there, too? (*Mary Magdalene steps out.*)

JESUS: Yes, Mary. What changes she made in her life when she heard the gospel! (*She goes to the disciples.*) She was with the disciples, learning and teaching. I was proud she was my friend.

YOU: And other women, too? Did you have other women friends? (*five to ten women gather around them.*) Oh, yes, many others, some for a life long, some only briefly. So many gave me their trust and love and support.

YOU: I always think of you supporting others, not so much others supporting you.

JESUS: Friends support each other, like your friends support you.

YOU: Yes, I have friends. (*Present day friends of You enter with a short blast of happy noise.*)

JESUS: Yes, you do. So many friends. (*Lines of women, costumed in many ages, ancestors, come toward You.*) You gasp at seeing so many women. Can you name them? (*You say several names, then Grandmother, Auntie.*)

JESUS: Family--what women in your family do you know? (*You greet each woman; actors come out who fit each description.*)

Friends from long ago, childhood friends--who are they? See their faces. (*Others who are YOU's age enter.*) Friends from places you have worked and schools where you've been together, clubs, groups, church—who do you remember? (*Shake their hands or hug them.*) Neighbors and some women you've met only once, cashiers at the grocery store and a server who brings you coffee, some forever friends and some momentary friends. Who is important to you? (*These friends could have on uniforms to distinguish them.*) There may even be some friends whose faces you don't recognize, women who you've made an impression on without even knowing it.

NARRATOR: Jesus calls you by name again.

JESUS: YOU! YOU! I had four friends who stood near the cross on Golgotha: John, my mother, my aunt and Mary Magdalene. (*Jesus crosses when the four enter holding the cross.*) Which of your friends would be with you at your end on earth?

NARRATOR: You stop to look over so many faces again. You see the faces of those who would be at your side to support you and love you. *To audience:* Name those who share a part of your heart. (*Each actor goes into the audience and holds hands with a woman, preferably someone they know.*) As you do that you are warmed in their presence, and love shines through in your mutual heart. As the women turn and leave with Jesus, you know it is not the last time you will see them. (*Women and Jesus turn upstage, and then turn around to wave. They start to walk off.*) Many you will see soon or relatively soon. Some you will not see until you reunite with them after you and they are gone from this world. They wave. (*They turn again and*

you wave, and you are left knowing you are friends. Narrator exits.
You is the last one to exit; she waves to audience.)

I'm still grinning at the sweetness that filled the stage that day. There were tears in the eyes of every Mom, Dad, and Grandparent, and Pastor. I wish I could have been in on every conversation that took place in every family car on the way home. How many Moms asked, "Who is your best friend?" And how many kids answered, "You, Mom." And how many meant it, at least at the time. Jessica told me she told her friends at least one time in their young lives that her best friend was Mom. Now she has a new BFF every week or so. Times change. Rules change.

SEVENTEEN

FOR LONELINESS, FRIENDLINESS

Make New Friends

"Love each other as I have loved you. Greater love has no one than this, that he lay down his life for his friends. You are my friends if you do what I command." John 15:12-14

Usually I take my car the seven blocks from home to the church as I'm always going somewhere during the day, but since Jessica needed it and I wouldn't today, I told her I would walk. I won't mind as the concrete walkway in the park goes by the river and then turns into a dirt walk through the woods back to the city on the other side. I start to day dream as I begin the walk that I have taken many times.

Sometimes when I walk this familiar path, it comforts me. I know it well. I feel safe here. It gives me peace, or it energizes me. Today is different. Today my alone-ness is loneliness—probably coming from the loss of my two good friends. It's part of grief. Grief comes even though I am surrounded by my dear family. The morning fog hasn't burned off yet. I know it will; it always does, but it's not something I have control over; I prefer control.

I walk by people who are busy chatting to their companions. I see children at play, happy to be together. I see others solo, but in their own worlds, concentrating, exercising, focusing on something other than me. I feel left out. The aloneness is thick, like the fog, and it separates me from the others. The aloneness is fierce, a strong wind blowing in my face that I have to push against to move forward. The aloneness settles on me like night, darkening the world around me and darkening my mood.

I look out beyond the fog and the wind and the darkening day for a friend, someone I love, even just someone I know, and I see no one. Then I see someone coming toward me through the fog. She, too, is pushing against the wind and squinting against the dark. As she comes near, I see that I don't know her. I turn my head away from her as she passes by silently.

I see someone else coming toward me. I can barely see him in the dark, but there is something familiar about him. I put my hands out in front of me, like a blind person, against the dark and the wind. I expect the man to be doing the same. But he doesn't. The wind and the fog don't seem to be affecting him. He walks quickly, purposefully, and directly toward me. As he reaches me, he takes my hands that I had protectively stretched in front of me. Then I know him immediately. It is Jesus.

He calls me by name. "Hello, Julia," he says. "I saw you walking alone."

"Yes," I say. "I'm all alone."

"No, you're not. I'm here."

"Yes, Jesus, you're here now."

"You're alone, but you don't want to be alone. Is that right?"

81

I say, "Sometimes I like to be alone—to think, to pray, to meditate, to do things I like to do best by myself. But today I feel the emptiness of being alone. And I hate that."

Jesus asks, "Did you choose to be alone?"

I answer, "No. I didn't choose. This being alone is the complete absence of a friend."

"Do you have a friend?" he asks.

I answer, "Yes."

"Is it a great friendship? Why is your friend not with you?" I put on a sad face, hoping he already knows the answer. Of course he does. Jesus asks, "When did you last make a friend?"

"Make a friend?"

"Yes, make a friend. See a stranger become an acquaintance and then a friend, even a great friend. When did you last make a friend?"

I shrug and shake my head.

"Maybe it's time to make another," Jesus says. I wonder if I can. "Instead of waiting for a great friendship to just happen, begin to share what you are thinking and feeling. You're doing it with me right now. Watch how the other responds. Can you visualize the conversation?"

"Yes, I think I can. I'd say something that I see about her, mention something we both have in common, like walking in the park, tell her why I enjoy it, ask her why she enjoys it—something like that—suggest we walk together."

"You see, you know how!"

"But I can't do that with a stranger. I'm shy. And I might get ignored—or rejected."

"You might. If you do, you can try again, can't you?"

"Yes, I suppose I can."

"And you can lean on the Holy Spirit to tell you what to say. The words will come. That's one way the Holy Spirit blesses you."

"You bless me, Lord, by being with me."

"And I will always be with you. You will never be without a companion because I can be your companion. But it's good to have a friend. I never meant for you to be alone."

"Thank you, Lord."

I am not upset when Jesus says goodbye for now and walks slowly away. I am warmed by the Holy Spirit that he has left with me.

It may not have happened exactly like that, but I can tell you it is the truth. Actually it happened through a cross between imagining and listening and remembering the words of the Bible and the words of my mother. My mother. She wasn't one for quoting the Bible. I had to wait until seminary to hear that. But she had a wisdom beyond me whatever age I was. She was not well educated. She said she had graduated high school, but the only time she talked about school was a story of trying to make a pair of bloomers in sewing class and the teacher making her take out the big, uneven stitches and trying again until the white cloth was black from dropping it on the floor. It was the only thing she ever sewed, she said. But she pinned up many a skirt for me and praised me for my sewing which I did from seventh to twelfth grade, making most everything I wore to school.

One day I needed a pair of brown pants in a hurry and, with no time to sew them, I ran to Penney's and bought a pair. She took one look at the fit of the store-bought pair compared to my homemade, and from then on she banned me from the sewing machine.

I think of what she taught me. Not cooking. She cooked about six or eight things total. You could count on her continuity. Most of it was just food. Except desserts which were always yummy. Never anything fresh. I never had a salad until I was fourteen and ate one at the neighbor's. Open a can; bake the same roast every week, of course—eye of the round—so Dad could have the same sandwiches from it every day in his lunchbox at the studio. Put together the boiled spaghetti with the flavor pack of spices and cans of tomato sauce. Stir it up. Then put it in the oven for an hour so every mouthful was mush and tasted the same. That's Mom's spaghetti.

I didn't mind. I didn't know any better. And neither did my mother. In the early days Dad asked her to make Jewish food for us, but she refused. He thought his mother was the best cook of Jewish food in the world, and Mom didn't want to compete. I don't blame her on that one. Wisdom. Besides, who was going to teach her? Dad was a good cook of his Jewish favorites: potato latkes, kugal, wrapped grape leaves. Anything else we could get out of cans and bottles and the deli. It was LA. We had the world's best delis. White fish, lox and bagels, chopped liver on rye bread. Every Sunday Dad would take me and pick me up from church; then we'd go to the deli and bring it all home, unwrap it and spread it all out on the kitchen table. Mom would run in, grab two slices of rye bread and her pot of chopped liver and run to the other room. She couldn't stand the smell of the fish. Every Sunday Dad and I would start out our feast with a laugh.

Memories. It's great to have some good ones. Especially ones of your Mom and Dad.

Some of my best friend memories are with my almost lifelong friend Susan. We became friends in the theater department in college. We did every show together; she was always the leading lady; I had some roles and did advertising and tech and even directed some. We never competed which was a good thing for our friendship. She has great beauty, a beauty that was perfectly suited to the era, long blonde hair and blue eyes. More importantly, she has the loveliest personality. She is energetic, smart, and funny, and lively, sings and dances, great at a party. She has more good friends than anyone I know, and every one of them think she's their best friend, including me (a trait my Aunt Millie had, too). Men and women alike think she's the best, and she is.

I've learned the better parts of my personality from her. Take a responsibility, and make it a joy. Everyone has something to make you like them. If there's something you really want, you have to work hard for it. There are some things in life that you just don't understand, and those you have to give to God.

She was in her late 50's with her husband in a new town far from home, and the two of them decided they wanted to do a triathlon. So they went into training. She found a small group of young people at church who wanted to do it, too—I think they just wanted to do it with her. Bike riding, running and swimming. They practiced two high action sports every day in rotation: one day biking and running, then running and swimming, then swimming and biking. Every day except Sunday, their day of rest, good for the body. I asked her if she won. She answered, "I finished." I was so proud. Her husband David put a congratulatory message on Facebook that said, "Who is this woman?"

It is to be expected, isn't it, that life cannot be so perfect. Of course not. They adore their three children, and they taught them well. But the unexpected sadness came out of joy, when their first grand-baby was born and died after three days. The birth had come too soon, the child's body was not completely formed, and her heart was not strong enough. There was no fault anywhere. The mother and doctors had done everything right, and still the baby died. The entire family was crushed. It is a big family of cousins and great-grandparents, and the pain was critical. I had no way to help. I was away at seminary and communicated through daily calls for a long while. Susan spent the calls telling me about the pain others had, her daughter, David, their grandmother—never herself. Eventually

I could ask more direct questions about herself. There weren't any answers. I had none, so I spent the calls listening.

I tend to talk a lot. Susan says its one of things she likes about me, that I tell a lot of stories, but that's just because I make her laugh. Before I was married and without children, I didn't have anyone to talk to on a regular basis, so I talked to the dog. And the dog doesn't remember if I have told him the story before. I suppose I talk to myself, too, although I don't know that because you don't know if you are chatting to yourself if there is no one around to listen. I had a church secretary who would talk to her computer constantly, in full voice. Sometimes I would close the door to our connecting offices, telling her I wanted to write or pray or make a private call when I really just didn't want to hear her voice any longer. Oh dear, now all of my secretaries are going to be insulted. Now with Mark spending long hours at the hospital, there are few long talks, and now that the girls are teenagers and don't have anything to say to their Mom, and they communicate only by texting anyway, I find myself talking to myself again. I'm not complaining. I'd rather talk with myself now that Mom and Dad are gone than be constantly silent, and as a pastor I seem to talk continuously anyway to a whole mess of people. I have to concentrate on being quiet at the appropriate times. I find that difficult, but I'm working on it. This book helps. I talk to the book sometimes. You don't mind, do you?

There is a rule in our house that's been in action nearly since our Jessica could walk. When Mom is in her office with the door a little bit open, you must knock and wait to be admitted. If the door is closed, locked or not, you may come back, but at that moment, you would not be welcome. The reason is that she closes the door when she talks with God, otherwise known as praying. She writes her sermons with the door open; she reads the Bible with the door open. In fact there is a family joke that says, "You can go in. She's just reading the Bible." The children used to say it without understanding the joke. They do now. Occasionally they would berate their pastor/ mother for falling asleep or closing her eyes sitting up in her chair while talking to God. The whole issue was very confusing. And they didn't know (and won't 'til they read it here) that it is even more complex when their father is added to the mix.

If the door is open a bit, the intruder can see the desk and the pastor easily from the space and can see whether her eyes are closed. If so, Father can slip in and close the door behind him, locking it silently. He can then slip across the floor silently and bend down on his knee by the pastor's chair, put a hand over her mouth softly or pinch her lips together softly and brush her cheek with his lips, causing her to open her eyes and close them quickly again frozen in her chair. The brush then turns into a peck, the peck a kiss, then an all-over-the-face fest of kisses, a few with licks, concentrating on the closed eyelids but not on the lips. When the pastor is sufficiently motivated, she reaches her arms around him and breaks away from his grip on her lips, intent to pull his head to hers and kiss his lips. He then has two choices: to kiss her lips or to break away before the kiss and slip away from her, unlocking the door as he chuckles, and slip out, leaving the door ajar and the pastor flustered. If, though, he has chosen to kiss her back, the picture changes, and the married couple may fulfill their appropriately lustful desires. Yippee.

It is so easy to adore my husband Mark. Not only is he incredibly handsome in the Nordic manner, 6 foot 2, with a shock of blonde hair even at our age, and still incredibly blue eyes, he has the sweetest most thoughtful personality. We are ying and yang. I am pushy; he is easy going. He is soft spoken and thinks before he speaks; I chatter. He writes thank you notes prolifically; I forget. When we walk together down the halls of his hospital, he is the one who people stare at, not me. He's the one who ignores their smiles and attention while

I say hello and try to remember their names, even though they don't know I'm walking beside him. He's fabulously smart, has a brain for business, runs the hospital like it's a corner drug store (I mean with simplicity—all the pieces work together easily), but he treats every patient like she's the only patient he has and he likes her best, especially the old ladies. I often tell him I can't wait to get old so I can have somebody treat me like that. Then he says, "Like what?" and kisses me with gusto.

Mark is the one I go to when I can't figure out what to do about the teenage girls we are raising or who are raising us. More often than not, he will say, "Don't worry. I'll take care of it." Then a few minutes later I'll look through the backyard window and see him with the problem child of the day squished together in the single swing whispering together. And giggling. I love it when Mark giggles. No matter what the situation. Sometimes in our very private times, he will giggle most inappropriately. It's a very low giggle then, like a cat who has caught the canary, as my mother used to say.

How my mother loved him. I could never tell her about a little argument we two had because before I even finished the set-up, she'd be on his side, and I'd be alone in the backyard. After we had graduated college and I was trying to decide if I should marry him, she told me, "How could you even consider looking at someone else when Mark is around?" When I was a teenager and going to church and youth group with the same kids all the time, somehow we girls found ourselves passing notes to each other on the back row of the church during the service. The first note said, "If you had to choose from all the men in the church for a husband, which one would you choose?" We voted 100% for our Sunday School teacher who was an intern at UCLA Hospital and handsome and marvelous and perfect. Finally one of us added to the note that he was already married, as if we didn't know. So the vote went around again, and every girl

voted for Mark, one adding, "Well. He's almost perfect, for his age."
I looked down that row at all the beautiful girls, and I thought, what
chance do I have? I kept saying that until the day we were married—
after, really. I actually asked him the next morning if he were sure
he had done the right thing. He giggled.

EIGHTEEN

Jesus to the Rescue

Searching for The Face

"So do not fear for I am with you; I will strengthen you and help you…For I am the Lord your God, who takes hold of your right hand, and says to you, Do not fear, I will help you." Isaiah 41: 10, 13

I was still walking on a path in the woods. It's a very pleasant woods and a crisp day. The fog was continuing to burn off, and as Jesus left in my musings, I noticed the sunshine and blue sky—pastoral perfection. I felt completely safe. When you are feeling that safe, all you need concentrate on is putting one foot lazily in front of the other, and the rest is pure enjoyment of the countryside.

Just then I passed a bramble bush full of thorns, and as careful as I was to step around it, somehow I got caught on a thorn. As I struggled to get out, I got more and more enwebbed in the bramble, stuck by thorns and stuck by their prodding. I saw the metaphor there. Time to bring me back to an age old thorn in my side. It must have been the thoughts of my wise Mother, who never said a bad thing about any person she met.

The more I fight against the thorns, the more I'm stuck and hurt and bleeding. I want to scream and yell for help, but I feel foolish yelling over a little thorn.

Just then I see a hand coming from around me. I don't immediately know the hand. Perhaps it's an enemy or someone who wants to hurt me.

I fight against the hand, screaming and hitting out and kicking. Then I hear someone call me by name and calmly say, "Julia, Stop fighting. You're alright. I'm here to help you." I recognize the voice. It is Jesus. I know the voice, but I hardly know what to do. I reach out through the bramble and grab him, holding on for dear life. I don't let go.

Slowly, he releases me from the bramble, pulling off the entwining arms of the wicked plant and pulling out the stinging thorns. With a soft cloth he wipes off the dots and drips of blood that are left from the thorns. He wraps me in a blanket, and he holds me in his arms. He is a big God, and I am a little infant. Oddly enough I remember the feeling from being in my mother's arms. I was a newborn then, being without the ability to help myself. I looked up into my mother's face, my mother who did everything for me, fed me, warmed me, kept me safe, just as I now look up into the face of my Lord. I have searched for The Face since I left my mother's arms, and now I have found it again in my Savior.

Jesus sets me down softly on solid ground. I am not a baby any longer nor a child. I am as I was before I got caught in the bramble, while I was walking though the pleasant woods. But now, whenever I get caught in a bramble, I can picture The Face of God and know I am protected.

Yes, but what do I do about the thorn? What is to be done?

Before I left for seminary the Presbyterian Church gave me a time with some people in the church to help me prepare. One of my favorite people who volunteered to be on my Committee (with Presbyterians, everything is a Committee) was the church Executive Secretary who not only ran the church but had worked for years with the pastor and had become wise in the ways of the church, and she was my friend. She said to me during one meeting that she had a concern for me that I was too tender-skinned, thin skinned. "People in the church think the Pastor goes around with a big target on his back (she meant "her back", too), and it's just fine to take any kind of pot shot at it that they want. You will have to learn to be more thick-skinned than you are." I never thought of myself as a wimp. In fact I was often called too pushy or aggressive or worse. If I had been a man, those descriptive word would have been strong, assertive and a leader, but alas, it was the 1990's. She was my friend and smart and experienced, and she saw through me. She knew that sometimes I was tearful. Sometimes I knew my way around. Sometimes I just pretended.

I never got sufficiently thick skinned that I didn't need to pretend. In three cases, I was chased out of three churches with major holes and slices in my delicate skin.

I'll tell you more about this committee later.

NINETEEN

FEAR OF THE UNKNOWN

Let Go and Let God: The New Bicycle

"Whoever listens to me will live in safety and be at ease without fear of harm." Proverbs 1:33

It was an idyllic childhood for me. It was like I was an only child. That sounds odd, as I had an older half brother, James, called Jamie when he was young and by us still. He was seventeen years older and had gone into the army after high school at seventeen just before I was born. I have always hoped that my birth didn't cause him to leave home, but I was always too scared to ask, and no one would tell me the truth anyway. More likely he was graduated from high school and on his own and made his own choice to join to fight the Korean Conflict, not called a war, though plenty of soldiers died. He stayed in the army 19½ years. As the story goes he punched out an abusive officer of a higher rank who then fell off the bridge they were building, and the punch cost him the stripes he had worked nearly 20 years to earn. I didn't hear any of those stories about my big brother until much later. He was my Lancelot. Funny, handsome, sweet, powerful, loving.

Dad had built him a private room on the backside of our big garage in the backyard with knotty pine on the walls. It was a labor of love. I remember that Jamie would come home on his furloughs and stay in his private room. I was let in on occasion. One morning Mom called to me to go wake him up—she'd made him a big breakfast. It was a privilege, and I knew it. I walked silently through his door, crossed to his sleeping body, whispered his name to wake him lovingly, and he punched me across the room head first, following me with, "I'm sorry, Jules, baby, I'm sorry" a dozen times. My head swimming, I ran from his room and in the back door of the house, not breaking into tears until I saw Mom. Then she told me the story, the story mothers have had to tell their children post-war, post all the wars.

In Korea Jamie had slept in wet mud puddles in the bottom of foxholes. I knew what a foxhole was. He slept with his gun and his knife under his head. That I didn't know. He had been trained to assume that anyone standing close to him to wake him was the enemy. In order to save himself, to stay alive, he had to come up with a fist that hit first and then grabbed the gun, while the other hand grabbed the knife. I had seen Audie Murphy movies. I knew what that meant.

Jamie came in the back door calmly, dressed for the day. He took a seat at the table in the kitchen. I watched for two or three minutes from a safe distance, and then I walked into his arms, where we gave each other a love only brothers and sisters who love each other more than they can express can say.

In those days Jamie was my Jesus. He had been through it all. He knew it all. He had a personality anyone could like, and the girls couldn't help love that beautiful face and that gorgeous soldier's body. He married when I was about thirteen to the most beautiful woman I had ever seen, with a sweet and lovely personality and an eight year old daughter for a ready-made family. The early years of marriage while he was in the army stateside were hard on them, living on the posts. Their first child together was a girl, as sweet and beautiful as her mother with curly dark hair and a perpetual smile. I helped to raise the child in her early years. At fourteen and without any worldly wisdom, unlike my mother, I was told that we were just particularly honored to have the baby staying with us for a while. Think how much I could learn about taking care of babies which I needed to know as I had no younger brothers and sisters.

When I was fourteen Mom's back had gone out on her, so she was required to stay in bed, flat on her back. That dilemma did not stop the plum tree in the backyard from putting out its ripe fruit ready to be made into jam, a yearly mother-daughter adventure. So that was my job. I remember feeding the baby a baby-food jar of her favorite apricots and applesauce in the highchair, stirring the jam on the stove and running back and forth to Mom in the bed gently giving me recipe instructions. I was so rewarded for it in praise from my Mom and Dad that the scene has stuck in my memory.

I rather got lost in memory for a while. I thought I was going to talk about the new bicycle. What brought it to mind was that walk in the park where so many things happened to me. So here's the mind story about the new bicycle. You must think I'm really jumping around. There's the story about the thorn and then here's one about a bike. You know they aren't real stories about things that really happened, for the most part. They are more like metaphors, parables. Here the one about the bike. It's a parable.

I have no idea how my head developed this scene as it is so outlandish. It's about Jesus, of course, and me, who could be you. The idea came to me one day while I was thinking of riding a bicycle-built-for- two. I had seen a couple riding one in the park, and I translated what I saw in wanting to be riding with my brother, his powerful soldier legs really moving that bicycle. The thoughts came out like this.

You are a child—maybe five or six—and it's a lovely summer day for playing outside. You have just received the best gift ever. The gift you had waited so long for was now yours—a two-wheel bicycle. Your three-wheeler sits by the door, lonesome and forgotten as you move on to new adventure. Here it is, your new bicycle. Your wise parent, concerned for your safety and anxious to teach you the right way, has put training wheels on the bike. You hop on for the first time. After a little jiggling back and forth from right to left on the training wheels, you take off down the sidewalk, as fast and free as you were on your tricycle. You put on the brakes. They work great, much better than coming to a screeching stop on your little kid's trike.

"I'm ready. I know I am," you tell your father after only five minutes of practice.

"Ready for what?" he asks.

"Ready to take the training wheels off!"

"Oh, you are, are you?" he teases. "If I take them off, there's no putting them back on. You're sure?"

You're sure? What does he think—that you're a kid or something?

You say, "Just one thing. What makes the bike stand up on just these two big tires?"

"Nothing really, Julia," your father says. "You just balance on those skinny wheels. When you feel you're going to fall off, then you sit back up straight."

"What if I don't sit up fast enough?"

"Then you fall."

"Where will you be?"

"Well, until you practice enough, I'll be holding on to your seat, running alongside, until you get your balance, and then I'll let go, and you'll be on your own."

"Oh. Oh," you say slowly as you realize what pain and humiliation falling can be.

"I think you'd better leave the wheels on a while, just 'til I get the hang of it."

"Whatever you say," your father says and leaves you to practice.

You head off down the sidewalk, rocking from side to side, rocking to the falling off point and then recovering. Recovering isn't all that difficult when the extra wheel stops your fall, gives you time to react, and then rocks you to the other side. You practice and you practice, for what feels like hours, and then you think you've got the hang of it. You manage to go the whole length of the sidewalk upright without bouncing off either side wheel. You're proud at being so able.

You hear a voice say, "Do you think you're ready?" You turn, thinking it's your father, but it's not. It's Jesus. He says your name, Julia, and greets you with his wonderful smile that says, "I am your best friend."

"Yes, Jesus, I'm ready. I'm sure I am."

"Shall I take the little wheels off so you can give it a try?"

"Dad said, if he takes the wheels off, I can't have them back again."

"But if you're ready, you don't need the little wheels. Then the adventure really begins. You'll be able to go fast, to places a bike with wheels can't go. You'll be growing up--and having new adventures. What do you say? Are your ready?"

What might the new adventure bring? You think. Am I ready?

So Jesus does just as he says he will. He takes off the training wheels. You get on the bike, and it wiggles a bit under you.

Jesus steadies it with his hand on the back of your seat. He puts his other hand on your shoulder, to steady you a little but more to just remind you he is there. You get balanced in place before you move, and then the two of you begin to take the bicycle forward as you pedal, and Jesus walks alongside. You waver a little side to side, and the front wheel is like jelly as you let the handle bars turn too much to one side. But in a short while, you get the hang of it again. You are managing to go forward in a straight line without wiggling or falling.

"Okay, Jesus. I got it. You can let go now." Jesus takes his hand from your shoulder. Just as he does, the bike starts to fall to the left, and it looks like you're going down, but Jesus pulls on the seat and rights the bike. You bring it to a stop.

"I thought you let go!"

"No, child, I let go of your shoulder, but I still had a good hold on the seat. You just couldn't feel me there. I'll always be there, holding on, ready to help you right the bike."

"So I'll never fall?"

"Oh, you might fall sometimes, but if you're careful, and you keep your wits, and you call for me to help you, I'll be there, and I'll try to make the fall as easy for you as possible. I'll never let go of your seat."

TWENTY

FOR PROTECTION, DIRECTION

Touch of God

"You are my hiding place; you will protect me from
trouble and surround me with songs of deliverance...I
will instruct you and teach you in the way you should
go; I will counsel you and watch over you." Psalm 32:7-8

"Stand at the crossroads and look; ask for the ancient
paths, ask where the good way is, and walk in it, and you
will find rest for your souls." Jeremiah 6:16

Sometimes I think my life is a constant journey. As a pastor I'm on
the road a significant number of hours a day, going to meetings other
than at the church, hospitals, visiting the sick, calls in the homes of
members.

In my younger days before and after college graduation and
the job that came after, before Mark, before kids, I tried to see as
much of the world as I could. There's a lot more left unseen. My
lifelong friend Brian lured me all over the world where he went to

graduate school or to live. I, too, was always moving from one place to another, from one adventure to another, from one experience to another. Though I loved the action, that journey caused me concern, stress, worry. I often did not know if it were the right thing to do. There always seemed to be roadblocks coming my way.

I remember a journey I once took. Shortly after I began, there was a roadblock. Big men in some kind of uniforms stopped me and told me to get out of my vehicle. "You must be searched." They were very serious and intimidating, but they let me go on my way. They gave me a warning of some kind: "Be careful out there. Behave yourself. Don't get into any trouble. Watch out...we're watching you!" One of the men in uniform reached out and touched me on the shoulder gently. His touch confused me.

They made me feel uneasy, but I continued my journey. The unexpected happened...it started to storm. Nothing big happened. The rains came, and I felt it plow powerfully on my shoulders. Soon they let up, and I felt their touch lightly on my face.

Whatever happened, I still continued on my journey...

until...a monster jumps out of the bushes at me. What does the monster look like? Is it scary? How big is it? How many heads? What does the monster do? More importantly, what do I do?

The monster reaches out and touches me, on my shoulder. I pull away...to safety. I continue on my journey. Am I hurt? Am I OK?

And then something happens that's the worst thing I can think of.

Am I frightened? Angry, confused, in danger of my life, hopeless? I cry out for help. And help comes. Jesus comes. "I am here," Jesus says softly. "I came to help you. You asked for help, and I came. First let me get you out of danger." Jesus picks me up in his arms and moves me out of the way of danger.

"Now," Jesus says, calming me, "tell me what is happening here." I do. I tell him. He listens. What do I say? I don't know.

"Are you hurt?" Jesus asks. I tell him no.

"Where do you want to go?" Jesus asks. I tell him home; I'm tempted to say Kansas, but I quench it.

"What do you want me to do?" he asks. It occurs to me that the wrong person is asking the questions. It occurs to me to go. And what do <u>you</u> want <u>me</u> to do?

Jesus affirms that I am right to ask. He says, "Good. Now you are asking rather than telling. I know how you are hurt. I already know what to do to save you from hurt or to let you experience it and comfort you—to come to stand beside you afterwards. I already know where you want to go and what you want me to do. You want me to save you from pain. You want me to give you success. You want happiness—all good things. And I want to give you all of those things. I also want to give you the journey—for your own good experience, for your own good strengthening, for the good you can do for others. It's not all about you.

"I already gave you this day for your journey. I protected you from the men in uniform. I brought them to help you, not to hurt you.

"I protected you from the storm. Sure, it was a roadblock, a trial, a dilemma, but you're still here, aren't you? You're still on your journey.

"I protected you from the monster. You pulled away and ran away. That was smart. Sometimes it is difficult to differentiate what is my touch and what is the touch of danger. You were wise. You get wiser every day with the experiences you have on your journey.

"I protected you from the worst thing that could happen, too. You asked for help, and I came. Sometimes I come to you without you asking. Sometimes you ask, and I come. Bidden or unbidden, I am there. I touch you, and you are safe...you are directed...led...you

continue on your journey. Sometimes you ask me what I want for you. That helps me help you. Like now. Now...I want you to stop. Turn to that road over there, and go that way. This way is too dangerous. It leads to things I don't want for you. If you listen to me and go down that other road, I will be able to give you more good things. This may be difficult for you. I want you to make a change away from doing what you want to do, to doing what his will and his good attitude want for you. Can you do that?"

I smile and agree. Jesus turns to go. Jesus waves to me and smiles to tell me he is pleased with my choice to go down the other road.

TWENTY-ONE

FOR SERVICE, CALL TO MINISTRY

You Do It Unto Me

If anyone gives even a cup of cold water to one of these little ones because he is my disciple, I tell you the truth, he will certainly not lose his reward. Matthew 10:42

The man with two tunics should share with him who has none, and the one who has food should do the same. Luke 3:11

I was a teenager, and I was in church without my friends surrounding me. I was sitting quietly, sometimes praying, sometimes listening, sometimes singing. We were singing a song about call:

"Here I am, Lord.
Is it I, Lord?
I have heard you calling in the night.

I will go, Lord, if you lead me.

I will hold your people in my heart."

During one of my listening times, someone came and sat down beside me. Even before looking at him, I knew it was Jesus. Often I pictured Jesus while I prayed. Often he talked with me in this way.

"Did you hear me asking for you?" I say.

"Yes, you are full of questions. What questions do you have?"

"I want very badly to serve you. I want you to tell me where to serve, how to serve."

"Ah, that is a good and real question. All true disciples search for where to serve. Often they find that place right under their noses. Occasionally they find it in the far corners of the earth. The important thing is not where to serve, but where to use the gifts that you have been given to best serve. First you must search for your gifts."

For a time Jesus listened carefully to me as I named my gifts.

Then Jesus said, "Let me tell you a story. A true story. There was a woman and her husband who were very well gifted in many fields, but I used them often as parents because they were especially gifted in the qualities that make the best parents. They had many children, seven. One died of SIDS as a baby and returned to the Father where she waits for her parents. They grieved over their loss, but I found ways to tell them that they had done their work as her parents because she was a special child, and they had raised her in love, even though they had her with them only seven weeks and three days.

"After raising their other six children and a foster child, I gave them the desire to adopt a baby in very great need from Ethiopia, one of the far corners of the earth as you know it. Immediately they knew that it was the right thing to do. They very quickly felt the calling I was giving them. They arranged with an agency in Addis Ababa in Ethiopia that was doing my work, to adopt a little girl I had waiting

for them. The child was extremely gifted as well in the many ways she would need to live in a cross-cultural society. For instance, I had given her the gift of tongues, in the sense that she would be quick to learn a new language, and the interpretation of tongues in the sense that she would help others learn languages as well.

"The caregivers in the adoption agency in Ethiopia sent pictures of the child to the parents, and they immediately fell in love with her. Immediately they knew she was theirs.

"In the various pictures with her was another child, a girl, who attracted the couples' eyes and hearts as well. The woman was warmed by her face, but she didn't say anything to her husband. At the same time the husband was feeling something for the other little girl, but he didn't express himself to his wife. The emotions just stayed within them, silently.

"Later, in the summer sunlight of a beautiful afternoon, the wife remembered an unexplainable experience she had had after her daughter's death and before the birth of her next child.

As she was dressing for the day, she had a very real and distinct impression for only a moment that there were several children in the corner of the room in darkness, with a young boy in front of them in the light. She didn't know how many children were behind him or why they were there, but she did know for sure that the boy in front wanted her to be his mother, and he wanted to come into their family.

"At least two years later their next child was born, a boy. She knew that her boy had been the boy 'in the light', but she could never gain a significance for the children 'in the darkness' behind him.

"There in the sunlight she suddenly had the same impression: several children were standing behind a young boy. This time, though, he wasn't in the light; he was light-skinned. And the children behind him weren't in the darkness at all; they were dark-skinned!

"The mother told her husband of her impression. Then like Joseph, with her gift of interpretation, she told him as well the meaning of her 'dream.' There were many black children waiting for them.

"They remembered the day they called Ethiopia to tell them they wanted two, not one. They also wanted the little girl with their child in the picture. The matron was curious and said, 'Which one? In the several pictures there were two different little girls.'

"The parents responded immediately, saying in unison, 'Both!'

"The story goes on. Before the adoptions were over, the couple had adopted six Ethiopian orphans and made them their children. And they continue to make others their foster children and to work in Ethiopia for the poor and those at-risk through a ministry they developed called Hope's Village. Hope had been the name of their baby who died...

I said to Jesus, "Jesus, what does your story have to do about my call?"

"There are lots of different kinds of call. I knew that this mother

106

and father were extremely skilled and gifted in parenting, so I knew they could handle more children, and not necessarily their birth children, so I gave them all those adoptive children. Plus... plus...there was lots of serious work to be done in Ethiopia with the relatives and neighbors of the children, starting with clean water, then protecting women and children, then healthcare, all the way to improving the Ethiopian economy, and I knew this was just the family to do it. And I was right, of course. I had a plan, a plan they didn't recognize at first, but it wasn't long until I had a complete buy-in from the parents, the family, the adoption agency, the Ethiopian government, their church, the hometown of the family...the list goes on...all starting out with a couple gifted in parenting...and my plans."

I was overwhelmed; even as a teenager I was overwhelmed, so I joined the team in a small way and got my church to join in. That's how I served that time. We just collected eyeglasses, cleaned them and sent them over. Even that small ministry met a much needed healthcare need. I didn't have to go to Ethiopia on a mission trip to serve that time. It was a blessing to be of use, and I was a blessing to others.

TWENTY-TWO

FOR CONCERN FOR OTHERS, INTERCESSORY PRAYER

Jesus, Help!

"Again I tell you that if two of you on earth agree about anything you ask for, it will be done for you by my Father in heaven." Matthew 18:19

"Love your enemies; do good to those who hate you; bless those who curse you; pray for those who mistreat you." Luke 6:27

"Therefore confess your sins to each other and pray for each other so that you may be healed. The prayer of a righteous person is powerful and effective." James 5:16

Pastors spend a lot of time in prayer. Most of my prayer time isn't formal, only the prayers I speak for other people, that is, when other people listen in. When no one is listening, I speak in informal ways, a few words at a time, just a name, a picture I conjure up of someone in a hospital bed or trying to walk with a bad leg or taking an ultrasound. Maybe holding a baby or a grandmother. I try to pray in my home office while I write my sermons. That works if no one is home. I don't usually call on the Holy Spirit to be with me. That is a given—bidden or unbidden, Jesus is there. Sometimes I ask for the Holy Spirit as I walk into a hospital or nursing home room or a home where someone is gravely ill or if I don't know what I'll be meeting. Usually just before I preach, after I've rehearsed my script a million times, I will pray, "I'll open my mouth, God. You talk." Same as saying "May the words of my mouth be pleasing unto you", but in my case, I sometimes forget vocabulary when I talk off the cuff, and then members of the congregation have to fill in the blanks, and that's an odd feeling of helplessness I prefer not to have. Recently as I was preaching, I was speaking from my script, and I had a quote, and I assumed an English accent without meaning to, so I stopped dead and said in the accent, "Yikes, I sound like 'Liza Doolittle!'" I got a big laugh, but I was taking a big chance because I didn't have the name until I said it—and I knew I didn't have it—but I counted on God to talk for me. That's what I mean by "I'll open my mouth, God. You talk."

The first time I remember praying, "I'll open my mouth, God. You talk", was in a committee meeting of volunteers who were supposedly helping me to get ready to go to seminary, to prepare me to be a minister. It was an odd combination of volunteers that looked good on the surface: the interim minister, the talented church administer/program director, a well respected woman who did high powered city-mission work, a local seminary instructor who worked in international mission and a man who taught junior high school. We had worked together about ten weeks once a week in a Bible study format. Early on they asked me when I thought I would be ready, and I gave a practical answer: I had started a high paying job with a friend, and I had committed to a year with him to start up a new wing of his business and to earn and save sufficient money from an obnoxiously high salary to take me through about three years at seminary. I figured scholarships should take me through the rest. The committee had agreed that they were willing to put in the year as well, for which I was grateful.

However, as plans of mice and men, and especially of God, often turn unexpected corners, my friend's business crashed, I was out of a high paying job after about four months and ready to get to seminary. I had done well with the savings, and I figured I was good for a year plus scholarships, and the seminary had already kicked in a sizeable cut from tuition. So I reported to the committee that I would be ready to go at the start of the year which was also the start of the seminary semester, about a month from then. Everyone had big smiles on their faces except the junior high school teacher who looked in shock and loudly shouted, "No!"

"No?" I asked innocently.

"I said no!" he shouted again. "We're not going to let you go. You lied to us, and you're not ready. We're not going to let you go."

The room went absolutely dead quiet. Without moving my head but only my eyes, I stole a glance at each person in the circle. Not one was looking back at me. I closed my eyes, and then I froze. If there were a time to pray, this was it. I had no idea what to say, so for the first time in my life, I said, "I'll open my mouth, God. You talk." This is what God said in my voice, "I know you don't know I'm supposed to go to seminary. But let me tell you that I know I'm supposed to go because God told me I'm supposed to go." Let me intrude here that until that moment God had never told me I was supposed to go. My pastor had told me. My aunt thought it was a good idea. My friends were not surprised, but I had not heard from God. Remember, I had asked God to do the talking, and these were God's words. God was telling me now. I continued, "So I would appreciate anything you could do to make that happen."

Only a beat went by before my friend the church program director spit out, "I can do that!" and then jerked her head to cue the pastor who immediately said, "I can do that!" in the exact same tone. The two of them jerked their heads to stare at the seminary instructor and then the city-mission worker who, in turn, repeated, "I can do that!" All of us then slowly switched our eyes to the junior high school teacher who lowered his eyes to his hands and sat silently until the chimes rang on the clock and then very softly murmured, "OK." We moved on with that new goal in mind, and God was in control once again.

It was a week later that the church program director let me in on facts I didn't have previously. The junior high school teacher had let the cat out of the bag to her that he didn't think women should be in ministry, and specifically not ministers, and he had made it his job to keep me from going to seminary and into ministry. He was trying to get her to join him in his fight, but he picked the wrong woman to recruit. There were many women in the church who were in some form of leadership, but I would be the first female minister. She was proud of me as the trailblazer and proud to throw boulders in his path wherever she could. Bless her.

You say, "I don't need anything for myself today, Jesus. Today I want to pray for others."

"Ah," he says, "a prayer of the righteous, an intercessory prayer, on behalf of another. Who is this other?"

You tell him. He wants to know more. You tell him how this other needs him.

It's as simple as that. You don't have to introduce your friend.

Jesus already knows him. You don't have to explain all the details. Jesus already knows the details. You can talk as much or as little as you need to. The prayer for your friend is for your friend's need, but it is also to express your Christian love for another. There is power in that love.

As you pray for your friend, picture him or her in the same way you picture Jesus. See her face. Hear his voice. Feel their pain. And then turn them over to Jesus.

Jesus says, "Give me the pain, the pain you feel for your friend. Give me your friend's pain, and give me your pain." Be sure to do that last thing: feel the pain yourself, but then turn that pain over to Jesus. Allow him to take the pain. It is part of what he suffered on the cross. He won't have to feel it again. He has already felt it. He can take it from you and your friend, and it won't hurt any of you again.

"Who else do you want to pray for? You've prayed for your friend. Will you pray for your enemy?" Ah, this one is not so easy, praying for your enemy. You know better than to pray that harm will come to your enemy. That is the natural thing to do, but you know better than to be in the natural. Jesus wants you to pray for those who mistreat you.

As you pray for your enemy, picture him or her in the same way you picture Jesus. See her face. Hear his voice. Feel the pain they caused you when they mistreated you. And then turn them over to Jesus. Jesus tells you, "No need for you to judge them. Only the Father can judge. And only the Father can punish. That dilemma does not belong to you. Be grateful that doling out punishment is not your duty.

"Now there is one more prayer to pray. You must pray for healing—for others and for yourself. You must pray that whatever this enemy has done to hurt you, you will now be healed and not

suffer from it any longer. Part of intercessory prayer is the prayer for yourself." He calls you by name and says, "Thank you."

"Why do you thank me, Jesus?"

"I will tell you. Whenever you pray for others, it is a jewel in my crown. It is one of the most tender, most humane, most unselfish acts a person can do. And I am credited with your unselfishness. You bring me glory. And I bring you love. Do one other thing for me and for yourself. Here we are in this big place with lots of room. We are alone together. But now I want you to fill up this place with the people you have prayed for. Start with those you have prayed for today.

"Now add those from this past week. Say their names if you can; if not, just see their faces. Picture them as you picture me.

"Go backwards as far as you can remember. Add face after face, name after name; bring them here and picture them until this place is full of those you have prayed for.

"Are you picturing them? Can you hear what they are saying? I can. All together they are saying, 'We call your name blessed...we call your name blessed.' The jewels in my crown sparkle and light their lives."

Jesus smiles at you...a broad grin...knowing he has made you happy and humble at the same time. He takes your hand and says your name. "Pray often," he says, "and in my name. Until then...."

TWENTY-THREE

For Prayer

Lord, Teach Me to Pray

"And when you pray, do not be like the hypocrites, for they love to pray standing in the synagogues and on the street corners to be seen by men. I tell you the truth, they have received their reward in full. But when you pray, go into your room, close the door and pray to your Father, who is unseen." Matthew 6:5-6

"...your Father knows what you need before you ask him." Matthew 6:8

"...he [Jesus] went up on the mountainside by himself to pray." Matthew 14:23

"One of his [Jesus'] disciples said to him, 'Lord, teach us to pray, just as John taught his disciples....Ask and it will be given to you....for everyone who asks, receives." Luke 11:1, 9-10

So many of the times in my ministry that I have loved best have been those with the children. One time I was teaching the Lord's Prayer to the fourth graders in our after school program. Over several weeks we had taken a line or two and talked about it in detail. Part of it was me explaining, but that was the smallest part. Part was some creative part. Once when we were looking at the first line, "Our Father which art in Heaven", I had the kids draw their impression of God the Father. Their responses were as varied as their number. One drew a picture of a long, gray-bearded old man sitting on a throne, the throne on a cloud. That was the kid who was going to the Catholic School, so the response wasn't a surprise. Some drew pictures of the sky and clouds, the home of God in Heaven, Heaven in the sky. A few, the most creative, drew fields and flowers and lovely, peaceful pastoral scenes. One explained that God was all around us.

Another day we talked about "Give us this day our daily bread." I asked what that meant. What did "daily bread" mean? Several agreed that we were thanking God for our blessing of food and asking for it as well, and someone said asking for food for those who didn't have enough, like the poor. One brilliant girl said, "Oh, oh, oh, I know! You know how on Sunday we have communion of bread and juice? That's our bread—that's Jesus' body. Jesus is our bread. When we ask for our daily bread, we are asking for Jesus to be with us daily... all the time. Right?"

I answered, "Of course, right." I never said wrong. They loved learning what the big people seemed to already know. And they always asked more questions than I did.

We talked about the kinds of prayer we gave and asked. "Sometimes you choose early morning prayer before you even get up to start the day. Then your prayer might begin with humming the hymn 'This Is the Day that the Lord Has Made' as you think the words in a silent prayer." Of course they jumped right in, praying

"This Is the Day." "Singing a hymn often helps you be in the spirit of prayer," I told them. "Or in the evening before bed, you choose 'Now the Day Is Over' as a prayer hymn to clear your mind of a busy day. Sometimes you choose to be on your knees, sometimes stretched out and ready for relaxation and sleep. Sometimes you go to your 'closet', that place away from the world that might be in your own yard, a prayer garden, a sunny window, a favorite big chair, some place that calls you to prayer."

"I like to pray in the bathtub," said a little boy. And his older sister preferred singing hymns in the shower. (Like me.)

The older kids like to begin prayer with their Bibles, reading words of the Lord, or a guided devotions book or magazine based on the Bible (especially the teens)—"whatever brings your heart and your mind to the Lord, open and ready.

"Then you begin. Sometimes prayer comes so easily. You know exactly what you want to say or think and words, thoughts, ideas and emotions just tumble out, ready to be in communication with Jesus. Other days your mind is blank. Then a little simple impetus is helpful." (I probably didn't say 'impetus'.)

This is what I told the kids. It's not original. In fact the first time I saw it I was at a pastors' meeting in the children's wing of a Methodist Church, and I scratched it down from a poster in the first grade classroom. "First say hello to Jesus. Call him whatever you'd like to express how you feel about him at this moment. Savior, Friend, Lord, Counselor, Redeemer--whatever is meaningful to you in your current spiritual state. (I doubt the poster said 'current spiritual state.') Picture Jesus. Picture him listening to you, hearing and understanding every word you will say, ready to respond. Say hello to Jesus.

"Second, after hello, say thank you. What are you especially thankful for today? Be as concrete and specific and simple as you can. Remember that you are growing a personal relationship with him. Talk to him about your real life. Tell Jesus.

"Next, after say hello and say thank you, say sorry. Is there a stumbling block that gets in the way of your relationship? Something you did? Something you didn't do and know you should have? Remember that asking forgiveness is an integral part of your spiritual life and critical to your growth. (Cut integral; change critical.) Say sorry.

"Say hello, say thank you, say sorry...now say please. What is it you want to talk to Jesus about? What are the desires of your heart that you need help with? Something related to your spirituality? Something as practical as it can be? Some need you need help with to figure out and to understand? Some friend who needs your intercessory prayer? Some divine intervention that only God can make? Tell Jesus what you mean when you say please.

"Lastly say goodbye. And speak your prayer in the name of Jesus Christ.

"Say hello. Say thank you. Say sorry. Say please. Say goodbye.

"Sometimes you don't need any pattern to draw you into prayer. You don't need a special place or Bible reading or the words of someone else to begin your prayer. You don't need music to set the mood. You just need to picture Jesus."

I hope your inner child is reading now. I hope right now you can picture Jesus. Close your eyes, and picture Jesus coming to sit beside you. You hear him speak your name. Nothing is so sweet as your name on his lips. Your God knows your name as well as he knows his own. You hear him say, "Talk to me."

You respond to his invitation. You talk. You tell him about your life, whatever is important to you at the moment...your worries, your concerns for others, your joys. All of that comes tumbling out. As long as it takes, Jesus sits with you. Sometimes you feel his arm around your shoulder; sometimes he takes your hand; sometimes he holds you like a child in his arms, on his lap.

Sometimes you don't talk at all. Sometimes you just listen. Take your time and listen.

Picture Jesus as he stands to walk away from you. You know that, whenever you call him, he will return.

TWENTY-FOUR

ABUNDANT WELCOME

Welcome! Come on in!

*"Whoever welcomes one of these little children welcomes
me; and whoever welcomes me does not welcome me but
the one who sent me."* Mark 9:37

*"You will receive a rich welcome into the eternal kingdom
of our Lord and Savior Jesus Christ."* 2 Peter 1:11

That children's sermon turned into a talk with you, didn't it. That's
how it is sometimes with the children's message in church. Some say
it's the only part of the sermon that they understand. It's a joke, of
course, I hope. Usually it's some older man being self-deprecating
and funny. I usually answer with something like, "Well, Jock, I wrote
it just for you, so you'd have something to take home with you." He
usually laughs and knows we made a connection.

With that in mind I once wrote a sermon making a connection
between adults and kids, about reaching the inner child inside us
to make a better connection with Jesus. And I used the idea of a

child coming into a group as a stranger and being welcomed. Our congregation is very big on welcoming people. Every week at the beginning of the service we say together as a welcome, "No matter who you are or where you are on life's journey you are *always* welcome here." With the idea that Jesus never turned anyone away, we push the idea that everyone is welcome. I like to remind my congregation that they can start with welcoming me, a female pastor whose mother was a Mormon, whose father was a Jew, who didn't become a mainstream Christian until a couple years before seminary, a big city girl from L.A.—all that is quite different from most people in my congregation. Half of them are Cradle Christians, meaning born into a Christian family and a Christian church, most into the Congregational Church that was big in this area in the 40's and 50's. 1957 the church voted to join the United Church of Christ and live by Jesus' principles of abundant welcome and diversity. Diversity is very big in our church. Everybody comes from someplace else, many emigrating from out of the states, from a different denomination, from a different belief system, even no belief system or anti-church beliefs. I'm curious to take a poll to find out, but that's contrary to the theology of diversity where all those things don't matter; now we are part of the one.

Jack and lots of others teased me about this sermon, saying that I finally wrote a sermon they could understand. The point of view of a child was so unusual that I was afraid many would say they didn't like it because it was different. Thank God for the Holy Spirit keeping them open minded. I used the opening line, "Picture yourself as a child--about six years old" hoping everybody could do that.

Picture yourself as a child. About six years old. Your mother has you by the hand, and you are coming for the first time to a new play group with several children from the neighborhood that your family just moved into. As the two of you walk through the gate and into your neighbor's big backyard, you see the children playing on the best swing set you've ever seen. There are swings on long ropes, and bars to climb, and an elephant that goes up and down, and a slide that comes down in a circle. It is a play set made in a child's heaven. The children are laughing and shouting and having a riotous good time.

You hang on to your mother's hand. How do you feel? A little scared?

The mother of the house comes out of the back door with a tray in her hands. On the tray is red punch and big chocolate chip cookies. You lick your lips. She hollers, "Kids...snacks!" Then she sees you and your mother. "There you are!" she says to you, and she gives you a smile that is a present of love. "We're so glad you're here. We've been waiting for you."

She calls you by name, and the children run up to meet you, shouting, "Hello! Welcome! Come on in!" A warm sun shines on all this friendliness and abundant welcome, and you slowly let go of your iron grip on your mother's hand.

"Children, would you like a cookie?" the other mother says.

"Yay!" the children say in unison, and the youngest child says to you, "You first! You're the guest! Our new friend!"

You take the cookie and punch from the tray. Was there ever a better day in your whole life?

[Then I changed the point of view. I didn't know how long I could carry the six year old metaphor.]

Now picture this. You're in church singing the first hymn, "Welcome, Welcome, Sabbath Morning." The church is full to the brim. That's the way you like it, so voices bounce off the walls along with the big organ and fill this place of worship. As the song comes to an end, you see a lone man in the aisle looking for a seat. There isn't one to be found. You think, "We can crowd together on our pew to make room for him." But just as you turn to the person next to you to ask him to slide down, you catch a whiff of the man. Is it sweat? Is it the smell of pot? Is it a bathroom smell? It gags you. You now see how this man is dressed, shabbily, in dirty clothes, with sneakers about to fall apart. You think twice about making room for him. And then you see his face. You know the face. It is Jesus.

He smiles at you and calls you by name. And then he says, "Thank you." And then he leans over to you and whispers, "You will receive a rich welcome into the eternal kingdom. God bless you, my child, for your abundant welcome." What do you do?

The church was absolutely silent. At first everyone was staring at me, for the longest time. Then people looked at their hands or reached for a Kleenex from the box at the end of each pew. I could hear the little "whoo" sounds as the Kleenexes escaped the boxes and were passed down the pew.

In the line to hug the pastor after the service, Jack had a frown on his face before he grabbed me in his requisite bear hug. He whispered, "Aw, Rev, ya did it again. I hate it when you make a grown man cry." When he let go, I chucked him on the chin.

TWENTY-FIVE

TEARS

The Desert

God puts every tear you have in a bottle, and when you need it, he will pour them back over you in the form of blessings. A folk saying

"He will lead them to springs of living water. And God will wipe away every tear." Revelation 7:17

"He will wipe away every tear from their eyes. There will be no more death or mourning or crying or pain, for the old order of things has passed away." Revelation 21:4

I am blessed. I am so spoiled, I stink. That horrible one-liner was used by my father when he did something amazingly nice for me, the "I" referring to me, of course, not him. He used it often as he was often amazingly nice, generous, sweet, kind, loving, etc., giving me a corsage of an orchid on Easter the same size as Mom's when I was four, teaching me to paint apple boxes for toy storage at eight, teaching me to read the nightly paper on his lap before kindergarten (for which Mom and Dad got in trouble as they had taught me to sound out words which was wrong in those days), reading *The Odyssey* with me every other page when I was in high school.

If I were to make two lists, one that was titled "Good, Beautiful Things that have happened to me" and the other titled "Bad, Ugly, Scary things that have happened to me" and then wadded up each of the lists and tossed them down the stairs, the heavier one would beat and that would be "Good Things". Silly way to say a simple thing: I am blessed.

I never would have guessed as a child that today I would be a minister with three churches under my belt so to speak, a fabulous family (I know, I say "fabulous" too much. It's a tiny sin.), and a slew of wonderful long-time friends plus parts of congregations who cared for me. Plus all those creative experiences with teaching, writing, art, theater, education, travel.

I think, though, that at this point it is only fair to clear up some discrepancies in the story. All of what I have told you is true. Remember that it might not have happened exactly like that, but it was nonetheless true.

However…however. Some of it is a lie. Not so much what I have told you, but what I was told and what truth I ignored in favor of love and joy. A sin of omission. For instance. I told you what a "fabulous" person my Aunt Millie was—which is true. What I omitted was that she was also an alcoholic. I have come to know enough about alcoholism to remind you that it is a disease that is not fully understood. Alcoholism is not a character flaw—it is a disease. My funny Aunt Millie would drink and abuse her alcoholic husband and also push around my dear mother when she could barely walk. And when my cousin asked my mother why she let her do that, she said, "I have to. I can't take care of myself." Pitiful.

But I must also tell you that in the last couple of years of her life—she died at ninety-one—Aunt Millie quit drinking. I don't know how she did it. I was far away, and I didn't hear of the change until her funeral. I can only imagine the exceptional difficulty for her, and I am proud of her more than anything you can imagine.

Alcoholism ran rampant in my mother's family. Out of nine siblings there were at least two sisters and their daughters who drank too much. There were also probably two brothers who drank too much, as those two committed suicide, over women, my mother told me once for which she was still angry. Luckily the gene skipped my mother and also me.

One more partial lie: it didn't skip my brother. Although he died a few years ago, it was a lifelong illness for him, probably coming out of PTSD that he got in war before that disease had a name.

Maybe this is a little lie, too. There is a rule for pastors who leave congregations no matter the reason, that they are not to return to the congregation. They need to continue with the denomination to keep their credentials, but they have to go to another congregation in that denomination to worship or to preach or even to visit. The reason is that it is best for the congregation to put their loyalty and focus on the new pastor and not to have the old pastor competing with the new. The new pastor has a very hard time of the segue if the congregation continues to bring in the old pastor to compete with the new. It is a wise rule but a very hard one on the old pastor. For years that person has put her focus and love into serving and caring for that congregation and now is not allowed to see her old friends. They have all disappeared from her life. It is painful. Even more painful is the last ministry, I am told, when there is no congregation that takes the place of the one she has left. That is probably why there is a rule that she must join another congregation in the denomination to keep her standing. Otherwise she might be tempted to change denominations in order to worship nearby.

I have a retired pastor friend who went through this difficulty and ended up driving across the state to go to a congregation of the same denomination. Short of the time spent in the drive, though, it turned out to be a beneficial move for her, and the new church benefited from the relationship that the retired pastor and the current pastor built very quickly and proved to be beneficial to them both as well.

I cheat. I sometimes break the rule of no contact with the old congregations. I still talk long distance every Sunday to Polly who was a dear friend of mine in my first congregation. Polly has an excellent relationship with the current pastor, and he knows we continue our relationship and often sends his best wishes. From the second congregation I have a good personal relationship with about eight old friends, but we carefully avoid talking about the current state of their church, and I only see them once or twice a year as the church is far away. One couple from day one took me into their extended family, and I could not bear to leave Mary and Ben ever. In the third congregation the kids' Sunday School teacher Josie and her terrific husband Ned are still best friends nearby. Alas, I could not do without them. Please don't tell on me. It would cause such a fuss if you did.

I once wrote a book full of guided mediations. I used the guided meditations in Sunday School classes, a part of an occasional sermon, in workshops at a Women's Conference, in book form for a few friends. I got the best results in small groups of clients from a Drug and Alcohol Abuse Treatment Center. One meditation that they liked best was about worry. (That's the first story in this book.) The clients were most often 20-something men who were addicts trying to get their lives together again. Their biggest problem in the Treatment

Center was worry--worry that they wouldn't make it through the program, worry that their families would be effected negatively while they were away with problems like not having enough money for food or rent or the kids would not be welcomed at school or kicked out of their friendships because their Dad was an addict, worry that they wouldn't be welcomed back to the family. Worries went on and on. I wrote several guided meditations for them that took away the worries by telling them to turn them over to God/Jesus. I remember one telling me, "I wish somebody had told me before I started at the Center." High praise. From the success of that story I have written this one for you to close this chapter and the book. It's about the bad things that can happen and what Jesus can do about them.

Jerry found himself in the desert. It was extremely hot...arid... stifling heat. There was silence except for the sound of an occasional insect. A lizard hid under the ledge of a rock. It was too hot even for the lizard to want to sun himself. He flicked his forked tongue at Jerry, to scare him away. It worked. Jerry was scared. Not so much of the little animal, but of what might be sharing the rock with him. Jerry didn't want to be there. He wanted to escape to somewhere safe. Just then great cracks in the earth opened at his feet. He jumped to safety, but his breathing came fast with the panic he felt from the danger.

He heard crying. He couldn't tell what direction it was coming from. It seemed to come from everywhere—under the ledge, and in the crack, and through the heat waves coming up from the earth. Jerry couldn't find the source. And then he realized it was coming from him, from himself. Tears were flowing down his cheeks, and the saltiness fell into the crevice at the corner of his lips. He touched his lips with his tongue. Nothing had ever been so salty. It was the only water for as far as he could see.

127

Jerry cried out for help. He cried, and he screamed. Thinking no one would come, he fell to his knees in prayer. When he heard his name, he looked up. It was Jesus. He jumped up and threw his arms around Jesus. Jesus held him while he cried. Tears wet his cheeks. For as hot as Jerry's body was, Jesus' cheek was cool. The penetrating heat was not affecting Jesus.

Jesus called him again by name, and then Jesus asked, "Why are you here?" Jerry told him what it was that had drawn him to this place of pain and depression, fear and solitude, death and mourning.

Jesus listened. He wiped every tear from Jerry's eye with his cool hand, and he put each tear into a bottle. As Jerry told his story, he quieted, and the air began to cool down. He could breathe again. Jesus took his hand and led him to a spring of cool water. He reached in and wet his hand and drew it over Jerry's face to cool him with the living water. What was left of Jerry's fear passed away.

He felt like himself again. He stopped crying. He felt ready to re-enter his home and his life. To Jesus he said, "Lord, I praise you and bless you and thank you. Only you could have saved me." Jesus smiled at him.

He told Jerry, "I have kept this for you." He showed him the bottle of his tears. "When you need it, I will pour them back over you in the form of blessings."

God's blessings to you. Amen.